Enid Blyton®

TALES OF TRICKS AND TREATS

Dear Marcus
Merry
Christmas
Ja.

Look out for all of these enchanting story collections

by Enid Blyton®

Animal Stories
Brer Rabbit
Cherry Tree Farm
Christmas Stories
Christmas Tales
Christmas Treats
Fireworks in Fairyland
Mr Galliano's Circus
Springtime Stories
Stories of Magic and Mischief
Stories of Wizards and Witches
Summer Adventure Stories
Summer Holiday Stories
Summer Stories
Summertime Stories
Tales of Tricks and Treats
The Wizard's Umbrella
Winter Stories

Enid Blyton®

TALES OF TRICKS AND TREATS

HODDER

HODDER CHILDREN'S BOOKS

This collection first published in Great Britain in 2019
by Hodder & Stoughton

1 3 5 7 9 10 8 6 4 2

A CIP catalogue record for this book is available from the British Library.

ISBN 978 1 444 94734 2

Printed and bound in Great Britain by Clays Ltd, Elcograf S.p.A.

The paper and board used in this book are made from
wood from responsible sources.

Hodder Children's Books
An imprint of Hachette Children's Group
Part of Hodder & Stoughton
Carmelite House
50 Victoria Embankment
London EC4Y 0DZ

An Hachette UK Company
www.hachette.co.uk
www.hachettechildrens.co.uk

Contents

The Magic Rubber

The Magic Rubber

ONCE A very curious thing happened to Keith. He was walking home from school with his satchel full of school books. He remembered he had half-finished a sum that rather puzzled him, and he sat down under the hedge and got out his exercise book.

He looked at the sum – and he saw that he had made a mistake in it. 'Oh, dear!' said Keith. 'I'd better rub that out before I forget.'

But he had left his rubber at school. What a nuisance! 'Bother, bother, bother!' said Keith.

A funny little man peeped out of the hedge at Keith. He was a brownie with a very long beard and the brightest green eyes imaginable.

'Anything wrong?' he said politely.

'Well, nothing much,' said Keith. 'I was just wishing I had my rubber with me to rub out something, that's all.'

'I'll lend you mine,' said the brownie and put his hand in his pocket. He took out a rather marvellous rubber. It was gold one end, blue in the middle and silver the other end. On it was stamped the brownie's name, TWINKLE.

'Just say, "Rubber, rub out!" and it will rub out whatever mistake you have made and not leave a single mark,' said the brownie.

So Keith said, 'Rubber, rub out!' and the rubber slipped out of his hand to his exercise book and rubbed out the mistake so smoothly that nobody could see where it had been.

'Excuse me a moment,' said the brownie. 'I think my telephone is ringing. I must just answer it.'

Keith was rather astonished to think that a

telephone should be in the hedge, but he could clearly hear a tiny tinkling noise. And, while he waited for the brownie to come back, a naughty little thought came into his head.

If I ran off home now, I could take this marvellous rubber with me and show it to all the others! Wouldn't I feel grand with such a wonderful rubber?

Well, it is always a pity when anyone does a mean thing. Keith didn't stop to think twice. He got up, flung his satchel over his shoulder and ran off with the magic rubber safely in his pocket.

He got home panting and out of breath. Nobody followed him. He had the rubber for himself.

I'll show it to everyone at school tomorrow, thought Keith. *I'd better not show it to Mother, because she will say I must take it back, if I tell her where I got it from.*

That evening when Keith did his homework he had a fine time. Every time he made a mistake he said, 'Rubber, rub out!' And it obeyed him at once, and rubbed out every single mistake without leaving a mark. It rubbed out ink just as well as pencil, and Keith was able to write out his geography lesson most beautifully. In fact, he sometimes made a mistake on purpose so that he could get the rubber to rub it out.

'You seem to be a long time over your homework this evening, Keith,' his mother called up to him. 'Do hurry up. What are you doing?'

'Mother, I've written out my geography and done six sums and made out a list of French words and I've drawn a map,' said Keith quite truthfully.

'Well, that's a lot,' said Mother. 'Come along down to supper now.'

Keith put his rubber into his pocket and went downstairs, very pleased with his evening's work. He didn't say a word to Mother about the magic rubber, but he kept feeling it in his pocket. It really was marvellous, all silver and blue and gold.

The next morning Keith ran to school in a hurry. He didn't go the way he usually did because he didn't want to go by the hedge where the brownie lived. He went a different way. When he got to school he called his friends round him.

'Do you want to see something simply too marvellous for words?' he asked. 'Well, look!'

Keith set out his exercise book with his sums so beautifully done, his geography lesson written out without a mistake, his nicely drawn map and his list of French words.

'What do you think of my homework?' he asked. 'Isn't it marvellous? Not a single mistake! I shall get top marks today.'

'How did you do it so nicely?' asked Bill. 'Usually you rub out about a hundred times and leave messes all over your page. Mr Brown is always telling you about it.'

'I'll show you how I managed it!' said Keith. 'Look – I've got a magic rubber! Here it is.'

'A magic rubber!' cried the boys. 'How does it work? Where did you get it?'

'Well, when I say to it, "Rubber, rub out!" it rubs out any mistake for me and doesn't leave a single mark,' said Keith. As he showed his friends the rubber and said, 'Rubber, rub out,' the rubber hopped from his hand and skipped to where Keith had spread out his homework books.

And my goodness me, in a second it had rubbed out all Keith's beautifully done homework! Yes – it rubbed out his geography lesson, his nice map, his list of French words and all his sums! The pages shone quite bare and clean. Not a pencil or ink mark was on them.

Keith stared down in horror. 'Oh, you silly, stupid rubber!' he cried. 'What did you do that for? Now I've no homework to show to Mr Brown, and I shall get into dreadful trouble.'

He did get into dreadful trouble. You can guess that Mr Brown wouldn't believe Keith's tale about a magic rubber that had rubbed away all his beautiful homework. And when Keith put his hand into his pocket the rubber wasn't there. No – it had slipped out and gone back to the brownie in the hedge. Nobody had noticed it hop-hop-hopping along the lane except a most surprised dog.

Keith had to lose his playtime and stay in after school to do all the homework again that the rubber had rubbed out. And this time his mistakes couldn't be rubbed out so beautifully, and he certainly didn't get top marks.

He is now trying to make up his mind to go and find that brownie again, and tell him he is sorry he ran off with his rubber, and he hopes it came back all right. I wonder if he will be brave enough to go and do that. Do you think he will?

Dame Roundy's
Stockings

Dame Roundy's Stockings

DAME ROUNDY was a clever old woman. She made lucky stockings of red, green, yellow, purple, orange and brown. Whoever wore her lucky stockings would be sure to have good luck for a whole day. So you can guess that Dame Roundy sold plenty, and there were always elves, pixies, gnomes and goblins in and out of her front door, coming to buy her lucky stockings.

But she would never sell her lucky stockings to witches or wizards. 'No,' she would say, 'I don't trust witches or wizards. They sometimes use bad magic instead of good. I don't want them to have my lucky stockings.'

So the wizard who lived in Windy Wood nearby had to go without a pair of lucky stockings, although nearly everyone else had them. He was called Wizard Shaggy because he had such big black eyebrows. He was not really a bad wizard, but he wasn't kind or generous as most of the people around were.

One day he badly wanted some lucky stockings. He had had weeks of bad luck, when everything had gone wrong that could go wrong. His chimney had smoked and the sweep wouldn't come. He had fallen down and hurt both his knees badly. He had had a bad cold and somehow or other he had made himself the wrong Sneezing Spell, and instead of stopping his sneezing the spell had made him sneeze two hundred times without stopping, which was very tiring.

'I simply *must* have some good luck!' said Wizard Shaggy to himself. 'I shall go and ask Dame Roundy to sell me some lucky stockings – and, if she won't, I shall get them *somehow*!'

So he went to ask her. But she shook her head. 'You know my rule, Shaggy,' she said. 'No lucky stockings for witches or wizards! So go away.'

Now, that night Shaggy went quietly to Dame Roundy's and listened to see if she was asleep. She was. He could hear her snoring very gently, and he grinned to himself.

He knew where she kept her lucky stockings. She had a big red box, and into this she popped each lucky stocking as soon as she had finished knitting it.

Shaggy tried the kitchen window. It wasn't locked. He opened it very, very quietly. He climbed over the sill into the kitchen. He felt his way to the red box. He opened it and took out as many stockings as he could hold. He only wanted one pair – but he thought he could easily sell the others to wizards and witches, who were always longing for them and could never get them.

He shut the box. He climbed back into the garden. He shut the window. Then he rushed off to Windy

Wood as fast as he could go. Hurray! He had plenty of lucky stockings now, and he would soon get some good luck.

But when he got back to his cottage he began to feel rather uncomfortable. Suppose Dame Roundy guessed he had stolen them? She might send Burly, the village policeman, to search his house. Certainly he wouldn't dare to wear any of the stockings for some time in case people noticed that he had a new pair and told Dame Roundy.

I haven't been so clever as I thought, said Shaggy to himself. *I'll have to hide the stockings somewhere so that no one will know where they are!*

He looked at the pile of brightly coloured stockings and scratched his head. Where should he hide them?

'I know!' he said suddenly. 'I'll go and hang them up in the trees! Their leaves are all colours now – red and brown and yellow and orange – and the bright stockings will match them beautifully. No one will guess they are hanging up in the trees among the bright autumn leaves!'

So out went Shaggy to do what he had planned. Soon all the coloured stockings were carefully hidden among the leafy branches of the nearby trees. Then Shaggy went to bed, happy that nobody would guess his secret.

In the morning Dame Roundy was amazed and angry to find her stockings stolen. She at once sent for Burly, the policeman.

'Shaggy the wizard came to ask for some of my lucky stockings yesterday,' said Dame Roundy. 'I think you should ask him a few questions, Burly.'

So off went Burly to see Wizard Shaggy – and on the way what did he find but a yellow lucky stocking, dropped on the path that led to Shaggy's cottage! Then Burly felt quite certain that Shaggy had taken those stockings and had hidden them away.

Shaggy pretended to be very surprised to see Burly, and he told him a lot of naughty stories.

'No, I didn't take the stockings. No, I shouldn't dream of doing such a thing! No, I wasn't out last night, I was fast asleep all night through. I certainly haven't hidden the stockings. You just hunt around my cottage and see if you can find a single one!'

Burly did hunt, but of course he couldn't find any of the stockings. He looked in the shed outside. He looked down the well. In fact, he looked everywhere, even up the chimney, but he couldn't see a sign of those lucky stockings.

And yet he was sure that Shaggy had them. Still, he had to go home at last, and Shaggy grinned like anything to see the back of him!

'Nobody will ever find my clever hiding place!' he said.

But that night a frost came. It was a very hard frost, and it loosened all the autumn leaves on the trees. In the morning the wind got up and blew hard. The leaves, which had been made very loose by the frost, began to flutter down in the wind.

Down came the leaves – down and down. Soon they were ankle-deep in the wood. A crowd of pixies, coming home from school, shuffled through the leaves happily.

'The trees are almost bare,' said one, looking up. Then he stared hard. 'I say – what are those things in that tree up there! And look, there are some more over there – in that bare chestnut tree! And some more in that hazel tree! Are they funny long leaves?'

Everyone stared. 'They look like stockings!' said another pixie.

'They *are* stockings!' said a third. 'Dame Roundy's stockings – the ones that were stolen. They've been hidden in the trees. Quick, quick, come and tell Burly and Dame Roundy.'

The pixies rushed off, and soon came back with Burly and Dame Roundy. While the pixies had been gone, Shaggy had suddenly noticed that all the leaves had fallen off the trees, and that the hidden stockings were now flapping and waving wildly in the strong wind. Anyone could see them!

In a great fright he rushed out and began to get the stockings down – and, just as he was doing that, up came Dame Roundy and Burly the policeman!

'So you *were* the thief and you *did* hide the stockings!' cried Burly, getting hold of Shaggy and shaking him till his hat flew off. 'Well, you can just come along with me now. I've got a few things to say to you!'

'Oh, I thought I was so clever, hiding the stockings among the bright leaves!' wailed Shaggy.

'I suppose you forgot that leaves fall off in the autumn!' said Dame Roundy, collecting all her stockings. 'Well, for a wizard, I must say you are really very stupid. Even a five-year-old child could have told you that!'

'What punishment shall we give him?' cried Burly.

'Let him come to me and learn to knit lucky stockings!' said Dame Roundy with a smile. 'It will be a good lesson for him to knit lucky stockings for other people and never be allowed to wear any himself!'

So that is what Shaggy *is* doing now – and he *does* have to work hard. Dame Roundy sees to that. If *you* want a pair of lucky stockings, you'll know where to go, but you have to be a good, kind person or Dame Roundy won't sell you any.

A Spell for a Puppy

A Spell for a Puppy

THERE WAS once a little girl called Joan. She had a great many toys, books and games, almost everything you could think of. You might have thought she would be happy with so many, but she wasn't.

She hadn't the one thing that she really did badly want – and that was a real, live puppy! Her mother didn't like dogs in the house, and would never let her have a puppy, or a kitten cither.

'Why do you keep saying you want a puppy to play with?' she often said impatiently to Joan. 'You have so many lovely toys. What about your doll's house? You never play with that now, Joan.

Get it out this morning and give it a good clean. Take it into the garden. It is nice and warm there, and it doesn't matter if you make a mess on the grass.'

Joan didn't want to play with her doll's house. She was not a little girl who was very fond of dolls. She liked running and jumping; she loved animals and birds. But she was obedient, so she fetched her doll's house and took it out into the garden. She went down to the hedge at the bottom, where it was sheltered from the wind, for she did not want all the little carpets and curtains to blow away.

She took everything out and cleaned the house well with a wet cloth. She rubbed up the windows and shook all the carpets. She polished the furniture and put it back again.

It was really a dear little house. There was a nice kitchen downstairs with a sink, and a fine drawing room and small dining room. Upstairs there was a bathroom with a bath and a basin. Three bedrooms opened out of one another, all papered differently, each with a little carpet on the floor.

It's a pity I don't like this sort of toy as most girls do, thought Joan, as she arranged all the furniture. *I wish I did. But people like different things I suppose. I love animals – I do wish I had one of my very own.*

Just then the dinner bell rang, and Joan went off to wash her hands and brush her hair. She stood the little house under the hedge out of the sun. She meant to go back after dinner and finish cleaning it outside. The front door knocker wanted a polish and the chimney wanted washing.

But, after dinner, Mummy said she was going to take Joan out to tea, and the little girl was so pleased that she forgot all about the doll's house out in the garden. She went off with her mother to catch the bus – and the house was left under the hedge.

When Joan came back it was late and she was sent to bed at once. She snuggled down under the blankets – and then she suddenly remembered the doll's house!

'Oh, dear!' she said, sitting up in bed. 'Whatever would Mummy say if she knew I had left my beautiful doll's house out-of-doors? I really must go and get it!'

She slipped on her dressing gown and went down the stairs. She went out of the garden door and ran down the path. There was a bright moon and she could see everything quite clearly. She went to the hedge – and then she stopped still in the greatest surprise!

What do you think? There were lights in her doll's house – and people were walking about in the rooms – and the front door was wide open!

Whoever is in there? thought Joan in great excitement. She bent down to see – and to her delight she saw that the little folk inside were pixies with tiny wings. They were running about, talking at the tops of their voices. They sounded like swallows twittering.

Joan looked into one of the bedrooms through

the window – and she saw, fast asleep in one of the small beds, a tiny pixie baby. It was really too good to be true. Joan sighed with delight – and the pixies heard her!

They slammed the front door at once – and one of them opened a bedroom window and looked out.

'Who are you?' they cried to Joan.

'I'm the little girl this house belongs to,' said Joan. 'I've been cleaning it today, and I left it here and forgot it. What are you doing here?'

'Oh, we found it and thought it would do so nicely for us and our family,' said the pixie in a disappointed voice. 'You see, we lived in a nice hollow tree, but the woodmen came and cut it down – and we hadn't a home. Then we came along by your hedge and saw this lovely house. It's just the right size for us, and as there didn't seem to be anyone living in it we thought we'd take it.'

'Well, I simply love to see you in it,' said Joan. 'I do really.'

'Would you let it to us?' asked the pixie. 'We would pay you rent, if you liked.'

'Oh, no,' said Joan. 'I don't want you to pay me for it. You can have it, if you like. I am very lucky to see you and talk to you, I think. I am most excited, really I am!'

'How kind of you to let us have it,' said the pixie, beaming all over her little pointed face. 'Can't we do something for you in return? Isn't there anything you want very much?'

'Well, yes, there is,' said Joan. 'I want a puppy dog very, very much. I have wanted one for years. But I have never had one.'

'We'll give you a spell for one,' said the pixie. She ran downstairs and opened the front door. She held up a very small box to Joan. 'Take this,' she said. 'There is a spell inside. Blow it out of your window tonight and say, "Puppy, puppy, come to me. Make me happy as can be. Puppy, puppy, come to me!"'

'Oh, thank you!' said Joan, more excited than ever.

'Listen, pixie. Don't you think I'd better take your house to the woods tomorrow? The gardener often comes down here and he might be cross if he saw I'd left my house in the hedge.'

'Yes, that's a good idea,' said the pixie. 'We would like to be somewhere in the woods. Will you carry the house there tomorrow morning? We'll show you where we'd like it.'

'Yes, I will,' promised Joan. 'Now, I must go. Goodnight, and thank you very much.'

She ran off, looking back to see the little windows of her doll's house lit up so gaily. She went up to her bedroom and opened the small box. She took out the spell, which was like a tiny bit of thistledown, and blew it out of the window.

'Puppy, puppy, come to me. Make me happy as can be. Puppy, puppy, come to me!' she whispered.

Then she got into bed and fell fast asleep.

And whatever do you think happened the next morning? Why, her Uncle Joe came to stay, and with him he brought a small, fat brown puppy in a basket – a present for Joan!

'Here you are!' he said to the delighted little girl. 'I know you've always wanted a pup – and you shall have one! His name is Sandy – treat him well, and he'll be a good friend to you!'

Joan was full of joy. She loved the puppy, and it licked her nose and hands, pleased to have such a nice mistress. She raced down to the bottom of the garden with the puppy at her heels. The doll's house was still there, and outside stood all the pixies, waiting for her to come.

'I've got my puppy, I've got my puppy!' she said joyfully. 'The spell worked! Now, I'll carry your house to the woods!'

She picked it up and carried it off, the pixies half flying, half running in front to show her the way. She put it down in a little glade by the side of a small stream and said goodbye once more. Then she and Sandy raced home again, a very happy pair.

And if you should happen to come across a doll's house in the woods, don't touch it, will you? It will be the one belonging to the pixies! They still live there, you see!

Briony and the
Naughty Fairies

Briony and the Naughty Fairies

ONCE UPON a time there was a whole family of very naughty little fairies. They lived round about the fairy queen's palace, and she found them really very tiresome.

'Well, I don't know what's the matter with those fairies!' she would say. 'They don't seem a bit like fairies, somehow – they don't care at all for beautiful things.'

Briony, the biggest of the naughty fairies, was the one who always led the others into mischief.

'Come along!' he called to the others one day. 'The dew fairies have just hung the dewdrops on all the grasses! Let's go and knock them all off again!'

'What fun!' shouted the naughty little fairies, climbing out of the buttercups they were swinging in. And away they all went to knock the dewdrops off.

When the dew fairies found all their beautiful work was spoilt they were very upset.

'You are unkind, Briony,' they said, trying not to cry.

Then Briony was sorry. 'I only did it for fun,' he said, 'not to make you unhappy.'

But he soon forgot all about that, and the next day began his tricks again.

'The sunset fairies have got orders to paint the sky pink and gold tonight,' he said to his friends. 'Let's go and change their pink and gold paint to green and orange.'

So all of them flew off to the hollow tree where the paint was kept, and in a little while all the sunset fairies' pots were emptied and refilled with green and orange paint.

'Now let's hide ourselves and watch!' laughed Briony.

They hid in a white cloud and watched the sunset fairies begin to paint the sky with the wrong paint.

'Oh, dear, oh, dear!' they cried. 'This is all wrong. The sky will look dreadful! Look at that terrible green cloud!'

Then they heard Briony laughing.

'We do think you're unkind, Briony,' they said, flying away sadly. 'You have spoilt a beautiful sunset.'

At last the queen called Briony and the naughty fairies to the palace.

'Briony,' she said. 'I can see that you must be punished. I shall treat you in the same way you have treated others.'

'Oh please, Your Majesty,' said Briony, 'I'm sorry, and I'll try to be good tomorrow.'

'You don't seem to care for beautiful things,' went on the queen, 'and what is worse you don't seem to care very much when you make others unhappy by spoiling what they care for. You will have to learn.'

'Please forgive us just this once,' begged all the naughty little fairies.

'I will forgive you when I see you are really and truly sorry,' said the queen. 'Now listen – each of you is to go out by yourselves and wander about for a whole week, trying to find a most beautiful thing to bring back to me. I will tell you what to do next when you come back.'

'Yes, Your Majesty,' answered the fairies, flying off.

Each of them searched hard for a week. Every day they looked for beautiful things, and because they wanted one for themselves they grew to love them, and to be careful of them.

'I'll choose this,' said one.

'And I'll choose that,' said another.

At the end of the week, all the naughty little fairies flew back to the palace.

'Show me what you have brought,' said the queen.

'I've brought a *lovely* thing,' said Briony. 'It's a bit of the pink dawn on a snowy mountain top.'

'It *is* beautiful,' said the queen. 'What have *you* brought, Melilot?'

'I've brought some gold from the heart of a crocus,' said the fairy. 'Just look; it's wonderful.'

'And I've found something lovely too,' said another. 'It's a bit of the blue-mist curtain that hangs over the hills in summertime.'

'Look at *my* beautiful thing,' said the tiniest fairy. 'I've corked it up in this bottle. It's the smell of the south wind in springtime!'

One by one each fairy showed his beautiful thing.

'Now,' said the queen. 'I am glad to see you love beautiful things at last, but I don't know if that will stop you spoiling other fairies' beautiful work. I'm going to make you feel what they feel when you spoil their sunsets.'

She went to a big pot of boiling water hanging over a fire.

'Come here,' she said, 'and put all your lovely things into this boiling water.'

'Oh, no, no, no,' cried the fairies, 'we *couldn't*! They would be spoilt.'

'You have often spoilt other fairies' beauties,' said the queen. 'Put your things in the water quickly. If you really love them, they won't be quite wasted. Something lovely may come from them still.'

Crying bitterly, the little fairies threw all their lovely things into the boiling water. Crocus gold, blue mist, pink dawn, everything went in, and was lost to sight in the bubbling water.

All the fairies watched their things disappear.

'Oh!' cried Briony. 'Now I know how unhappy we must have made other fairies when we spoilt their lovely work!'

Suddenly a glorious scent came from the bubbling

water. It spread through all the palace and all the garden.

'What is it?' asked the fairies, sniffing at the pot wonderingly.

'I told you your beautiful things wouldn't be wasted,' said the queen. 'They have made one of the loveliest perfumes in the world.'

'How glorious it is!' cried Briony.

'Yes. Now, you have learnt your lesson,' said the queen, 'and I am going to give you work to do. Take this perfume you have made, and put a little into the heart of all the summer roses. They look so beautiful that I want them to smell beautiful too.'

And now Briony and the other little fairies give the roses the glorious smell they have. No flower smells *quite* so lovely – but then no other flower has its perfume made of such wonderful things!

The Fairy Kitten

The Fairy Kitten

THERE WAS once a little boy called John. He lived with his mother and father in a lovely cottage at the edge of the woods. Usually he was a happy little boy, who laughed and played all day in the sunshine, but just lately he had been very unhappy because his little grey kitten had run away and got lost.

John had looked everywhere for her – in the house, in the garden, in the summerhouse, in the garage and by the road.

'She may have run into the woods,' said his mother. 'Go and see if you can find her there, John.'

So off John went to the woods where primroses and

celandines were flowering, and where the silver pussy willow shone pale and soft in the warm spring sun.

But his kitten was nowhere to be found, and John could have cried with disappointment. He had so loved playing with her and was sure he would never find another kitten that was as pretty as she was.

Suddenly he stopped still and listened. Was that a mew that he heard? Surely it was!

The noise came again softly, very high and quiet – not exactly like a mew, but John couldn't think what else it might be. He began looking about to see where the noise came from. It sounded as though it came from somewhere low down.

Yes, it came from the middle of a prickly gorse bush! Surely his poor little kitty couldn't be in there.

'Kitty! Kitty!' he called, peeping into the bush.

A little, high voice answered him. 'Oh, help me, please. I'm caught in the prickles!'

John was so surprised to hear the tiny voice that he could hardly speak. 'Who are you?' he asked at last.

'I'm a pixie piper,' said the little voice. 'The wind blew me right off my feet and landed me here, and I can't get out! Will you help me?'

'A pixie!' John said excitedly. 'Yes, I'll help you! I've never seen a pixie before! But, oh, my! It's rather prickly!'

He put his hands right into the gorse bush and pressed back the branches. There in the middle was a tiny pixie, dressed in red and yellow. Carefully John lifted him out of the bush and set him down on the ground.

'Oh, thank you!' cried the pixie. 'You are kind to help me, but look at your poor hands. They are covered in scratches and scrapes. And why do you look so unhappy?'

'I'm upset because I've lost my kitten,' John said sadly, and told the little pixie all about it.

'Dear, dear, that's very sad!' said the pixie piper. 'But don't worry, I'll help you. I think I know where your kitten may be. The fairies love kittens. If they've found yours, they'll have changed her into a fairy kitten. She won't be very far away, but we will have to use some pixie magic to find her. Have you ever seen a fairy kitten?'

'No, but I would love to,' said John excitedly. 'Where are they kept?'

'There're plenty over there!' laughed the pixie piper, pointing to a big pussy willow.

John looked. He could only see a bush with soft, silvery buds growing all over it.

The pixie took up his pipe, and softly he began to play a lovely tune, looking at the pussy willow bush all the time.

John looked too and he saw a wonderful sight – so wonderful he could hardly believe his eyes! For the silver pussy willow buds had changed into tiny, furry kittens, and one by one they all scrambled down the branches to the ground and ran up to the piper.

They danced and frisked round him, and ran after their little tails, for all the world like real kittens.

The piper stopped playing on his pipe. 'Now,' he said, 'you have to find your kitten. Which one is she? Quick! Can you see her? You must find her before they all go back to the tree and turn into pussy willow buds again!'

John ran after them, and picked up a little, silvery kitten small enough to fit into a nutshell. He had found his kitty!

Then he watched the others climb up the branches and one by one turn into soft, silvery buds again!

The piper blew his pipe once more, and John's kitten grew bigger and bigger until it was just the right size.

'There you are!' said the pixie. 'Don't tell anyone it's a fairy kitten. They won't believe you. Thank you for helping me, and I'm glad I've been able to help you in return. Goodbye.'

He vanished and left John alone with his fairy kitten. He ran home as fast as he could.

'Why, John!' cried his mother. 'So you've found

your kitty after all! I am glad!'

John told heaps of people how he found his fairy kitten, but the pixie was right – nobody believed him. Not even his best friend Robert.

He didn't mind. He knew what nobody else did – and that was where fairy kittens come from!

And next time you see a pussy willow, have a good look at it. I think you will say it's no wonder the fairies made kittens from such soft, furry buds!

The Talking Teapot

The Talking Teapot

ONCE UPON a time when Dimble-Dumble was walking across the common he saw a yellow teapot sitting in a gorse bush. The pixie was very surprised, for teapots do not usually sit in bushes.

It was a very nice teapot. Dimble-Dumble looked at it all round. It wasn't cracked, like the one he had at home. Its spout wasn't broken either. It was a very good teapot, and there was nothing the matter with it at all.

'Mine's very old,' said Dimble-Dumble. 'Mine is a disgraceful teapot. This one is a good one, and a lovely colour. I shall take it home with me.'

Now that was naughty of him, because he knew quite well that it must belong to someone. In fact, he felt certain that it belonged to the Yellow Gnome who lived not far away, and had yellow tables and chairs, yellow plates and cups, and probably a yellow teapot to match. But Dimble-Dumble wouldn't think of that. He wanted the teapot, and he meant to have it.

So he lifted it out of the gorse bush and put it under his coat. He ran all the way home with it, and when he got there he took the teapot out and looked at it. It certainly was a very fine one. Dimble-Dumble took down his old teapot and threw it on the floor, where it broke into a hundred pieces.

'There!' he said. 'Now you can go into the dustbin, old teapot. You're done for! I'll use my new yellow teapot, and make everyone very jealous!'

He put it up on the shelf, and then cleared away the broken pieces of the old teapot. As he was doing this, his friend Peter Pie came in.

'I say, Dimble-Dumble,' he said. 'Will you lend me fifty pence till tomorrow?'

Now Dimble-Dumble hated lending anybody anything. So he shook his head.

'I haven't even ten pence!' he said.

Then something queer happened. A loud, deep voice suddenly spoke in the pixie's kitchen.

'Dimble-Dumble's mean!' said the voice. 'Ho, mean Dimble-Dumble!'

The pixie and his friend looked all around in surprise. There was no one there at all. Dimble-Dumble went red, for he knew that the voice spoke the truth. He *was* being mean.

'Ho!' began the voice again. 'Ho! Dimble-Dumble's mean!'

The pixie hurriedly took ten pence from his pocket and gave it to his friend.

'Here you are,' he said. 'Now run away, because I'm busy.'

Peter Pie went out, much astonished. As soon as he

had gone, Dimble-Dumble had a good hunt around his kitchen to see who had spoken. He felt certain that some gnome or elf must be hiding there. But he could find nobody. The voice didn't speak again, but just as he passed the shelf where he kept his china he heard a deep chuckle. Dimble-Dumble hunted all along the shelf, but he still couldn't see anyone. He didn't for one minute guess that it was the yellow teapot!

After a time he gave it up and began to get his dinner ready. Soon there came a knock at the door, and a grey rabbit looked in.

'Dimble-Dumble, could you come and help me to pick my peas?' asked Bobtail the rabbit. 'I'm going to do them this afternoon. I'd be very glad of your help.'

Now it was a hot day, and Dimble-Dumble didn't want to work hard. So he shook his head.

'I'm sorry,' he said. 'But I'm afraid I can't.'

Then the loud, deep voice spoke again.

'Dimble-Dumble's lazy,' said the voice. 'Ho, lazy Dimble-Dumble!'

The rabbit stared round in surprise, but could see no one. The pixie went very red.

'I'll come and help you this afternoon, Bobtail,' he said in a hurry. 'Now run off, for I'm busy!'

The rabbit went away, very puzzled. Dimble-Dumble glared round his kitchen, but it was no use. He could *not* see who had spoken. The yellow teapot chuckled deeply, and made him jump – but still he didn't guess where the voice came from.

He ate his dinner, and then went off to help Bobtail to pick his peas. After that he came home again, and began to get ready for a tea party he was having that afternoon. He buttered some biscuits, iced some buns, made some jam sandwiches and took a ginger cake out of a tin. Then he set out plates, cups and saucers, took down the yellow teapot and put the kettle on to boil. By the time four o'clock came he was quite ready for his visitors.

In they came, Peter Pie and Pipkin, Gillie and Poppo, Chiffle-Chuffle and Tiptoe. They said good afternoon politely, and sat down to tea. Dimble-Dumble put some tea into the yellow teapot, poured boiling water in and the tea was made.

Soon they were all eating and talking merrily. Pipkin asked Dimble-Dumble where he had got his lovely new teapot from.

'It was a birthday present,' said Dimble-Dumble untruthfully, for he didn't want to say how he had found it.

'Dimble-Dumble's a storyteller!' said the teapot in a loud, deep voice. 'Ho, storytelling Dimble-Dumble!'

Nobody knew where the voice had come from. Everyone except the pixie thought that one of the guests at the table had spoken the strange words. They looked at one another in silence, wondering who it was.

'Ho,' began the voice again, 'Dimble-Dumble's a storyteller!'

'I found the teapot in a bush,' said Dimble-Dumble

quickly. 'It wasn't a birthday present. Don't let's talk about it any more.'

So his guests politely changed the subject and talked about other things. But the teapot wouldn't let them. It began to talk too, and it had such a very loud voice that it drowned everyone else.

'DIMBLE-DUMBLE IS MEAN,' it said. 'HO, DIMBLE-DUMBLE IS LAZY TOO AND DIMBLE-DUMBLE TELLS STORIES! HO, MEAN DIMBLE-DUMBLE, LAZY DIMBLE-DUMBLE, STORYTELLING DIMBLE-DUMBLE!'

'Who's saying all these things?' asked Peter Pie in great surprise.

'*I'm* not!' said Pipkin.

'Nor am I!' said Gillie.

'And *we're* not!' said Poppo, Chiffle-Chuffle and Tiptoe, all together.

'HO, HO!' chuckled the teapot, and it waggled its spout at them all. 'HO, HO!'

'Look! It's the teapot!' cried everyone. 'It's alive! Ooh! It's a magic teapot! Dimble-Dumble, how foolish you were to take it from the bush when it didn't belong to you!'

The little pixie was very miserable. He sat and looked at the teapot, wondering what it was going to say next. He didn't have to wait long, for it began to say all sorts of unkind things about him, and he went very red indeed, for most of them were true.

His friends soon went away, for the tea party was quite spoilt. Dimble-Dumble was left alone with the teapot, which began to make faces at him. It was a very ill-behaved pot.

'I'll go and ask the Yellow Gnome if it's his,' said Dimble-Dumble. 'Then perhaps he will have it back.'

So off he went and knocked at the door of the Yellow Gnome's bright yellow house. The gnome himself came to the door, and asked what the pixie wanted.

'Yellow Gnome,' began Dimble-Dumble, 'I found a yellow teapot in a gorse bush this morning, and took it home. I know it was very wrong of me. It is a very rude teapot, and says all sorts of unkind things. Will you please take it back?'

The Yellow Gnome slapped his knees, threw back his head and laughed a very loud laugh. When he had finished he shook his head.

'No,' he said. '*I* don't want it back! I threw it away because it said such rude things about *me*! You keep it, Dimble-Dumble! Much good may it do you!'

He slammed the door, and poor Dimble-Dumble went home wishing hard that he hadn't touched that teapot.

I'll smash it to pieces, he thought. *Then that will be the end of it!*

So when he got home he took hold of the teapot and flung it hard on the ground. But it didn't break! Instead, it bounced high into the air and hit the pixie on the nose!

He couldn't break it however he tried. Even when he hit it with a hammer it wouldn't break. So then he took it to the bottom of his garden and threw it away as far as he could. But it came back! It hopped up the garden path, in at the kitchen door and put itself in the sink to be washed. Whatever was Dimble-Dumble to do?

He began to cry. He tried to break the teapot again. He put it into the dustbin, but it threw off the lid and came back to the kitchen. He tried to drown it, but it simply loved the water and bobbed up and down like a boat.

So in the end the poor little pixie had to wash it, and put it back on the shelf.

'Ho, ho!' it said. 'Ho, ho!' And then with another deep chuckle it went to sleep.

But what a nuisance it was to Dimble-Dumble all the rest of the week! Every time he did anything mean or greedy, selfish or horrid, the teapot spoke about it. There was no stopping it,' and it had such a loud voice that everyone heard what it said.

Soon Dimble-Dumble found that the only way to

stop it talking was to be careful never to do anything wrong or horrid. If he told the truth, was helpful and kind, and never did anything mean, the teapot was silent. It only spoke when it could say something unkind. There it sat on the shelf beside a new blue teapot, which the pixie had bought because he wouldn't use the yellow one.

Then one day Dimble-Dumble had an idea.

'I found it in a gorse bush!' he said. 'If I throw it into one, perhaps it will stay there! When the Yellow Gnome threw it there it stayed, and didn't go back to him. Perhaps it will stop there if *I* throw it into a prickly gorse bush!'

He took the teapot and went to the common. He chose a very big, prickly bush and then threw the teapot right into the middle of it. It tried to get out, but it couldn't.

'Ha!' said the pixie in delight. 'Ha! Mean teapot, unkind teapot, horrid teapot! Stay there until someone else finds you!'

He hurried home, singing happily. Oh, it was lovely to have got rid of that nasty talking teapot!

But it's taught me a few lessons, thought Dimble-Dumble, putting the kettle on to boil. *It's taught me to tell the truth, to be unselfish and not to be lazy. So really I ought to be grateful to it, though it* was *a horrid teapot! I wonder who will find it. Well, they'd better leave it alone, or they will be very sorry!*

Nobody has found it yet, because the gorse bush is very thick and prickly – but if you *should* happen to see a yellow teapot on the common, take my advice and leave it alone!

The Brownies' Party

The Brownies' Party

GEORGE HAD been playing with his railway in the garden. He had a great many lines, and he had made a big loop of them all round the lilac bush, and had sent his engine and long line of trucks round and round it. It was such fun. He was sorry when his mother called him in to tea.

'Coming, Mother!' he shouted. 'I'll leave my lines now, and put them away after tea.'

But while he was at his tea, two little people found his lines and the train, and looked at them in delight. They were two brownies, Snip and Snap.

'I say!' said Snap. 'If we could borrow these lines,

we could solve our difficulty, Snip!'

'We could,' said Snip. 'Let's!'

'We'll ask the boy if we may,' said Snap.

'Let's!' said Snip. So, when George came back after tea, he was most surprised to see two small brownies waiting for him.

'Hallo!' he said. 'Who are you?'

'Snip and Snap, two brownies,' said Snip. 'We are in a great difficulty, and you can help us.'

'Tell me,' said George, feeling most excited, for it was rare to see brownies.

'It's like this,' said Snap. 'We are giving a party in the garden shed tonight – and we have all the plates, cups, saucers, dishes, cakes, biscuits, sweets, lemonade and everything in our little house on the other side of the hedge at the bottom of your garden.'

'And unfortunately it has been raining hard lately,' went on Snip, 'so the path from our house to your garden shed is very muddy.'

'And we keep slipping on it,' said Snap. 'So we are

very much afraid that when we carry all our china and party things along the path we shall fall and break them.'

'And we wondered if we might borrow your railway lines and train,' said Snip. 'Then we could lay the lines from our house to the garden shed and back, and let your trucks carry all our cups and saucers and cakes and things quickly and safely.'

'So will you lend it to us if we take great care of it?' asked Snap.

'Oh!' said George in the greatest delight. 'Fancy my train being used like that! What fun! Of course I'll lend it to you – if you'll let me come to the party.'

'Certainly,' said Snap, and he handed George an invitation card with a picture of brownies at the top. 'We shall be very pleased to see you.'

Well, think of that! Did you ever hear of such a thing in your life! It wasn't long before George and the two brownies had taken the lines and had neatly put them together again in another place. George saw the brownies' house on the other side of the hedge – so cunningly hidden in the hawthorn that no one would ever have thought it was there! The railway lines were laid by their house, through a hole in the hedge and then up the muddy path to the garden shed and right inside. The lines then looped right back again to the brownies' house. There were just enough.

What fun they had! George helped all he could, and it was thrilling to put the cups, saucers, plates, bags of buns and cakes, biscuits and bottles of lemonade on the train, wind it up and then see it going gaily through the gap in the hedge and up the garden path right into the garden shed!

When it arrived there George stopped it, and Snip unloaded the carriages, setting everything neatly out on the table. Then George started up the engine again and off it chuffed down the path once more, round the loop and back to Snap, who loaded up the carriages again.

Not a single thing was broken! Not a drop of lemonade was spilt! The brownies were so delighted.

'I'll leave my train here – and the lines,' said George. 'You can put the dirty things on the train then, when the party is over, and let it carry them back to your house for you.'

The party was a great success! George went, of course – though he had to go in his pyjamas and dressing gown, because it was held late at night! But none of the brownies seemed to think he was dressed rather queerly for a party, and when they heard about his train and how he had lent his lines to help Snip and Snap they all swarmed outside to see the wonderful railway.

And then, of course, they wanted to ride on it themselves – so the trucks were soon full of laughing brownies, all having a perfectly splendid time riding in the train round and round the big loop-line.

George said goodbye to everyone when the party was over, and then helped Snip to pile the dirty things in the trucks again, and the train chuffed off to Snap, who unloaded them and put them in his little sink to wash up the next day.

'Now you must say good night!' said the brownies, when everything was done. 'We are so very grateful to you, George. Come and see us whenever you like. You can leave your lines and train here till tomorrow, if you like, for they will be quite safe. The sky is clear and there will be no rain.'

So George ran back to bed, the happiest little boy in the world that night. He had been to a brownie party!

The next day he took up his lines and put them safely away, for it really looked as if it might rain. Then he went to call on Snip and Snap and found them very busy washing up.

'Come in and play with us whenever it rains and you can't play in the garden,' said Snip. 'We'd like to be your friends!'

So now when it's rainy nobody can imagine where George gets to! But we'd know where to look for him, wouldn't we – in the brownies' house on the other side of the hedge! Lucky, lucky George!

Fee-Fie-Fo the Goblin

Fee-Fie-Fo the Goblin

NOBODY KNEW where Fee-Fie-Fo came from, for he suddenly appeared one night with a barrow on which were all his belongings, and went to live in Twisty Cottage in the middle of Ten O'Clock Village.

The other little folk were quite ready to make friends with him – but they soon found that Fee-Fie-Fo was a bad friend and a worse enemy! He was mean and stingy, cruel and dishonest, and he knew such a lot of magic that soon the folk of Ten O'Clock Village were very much afraid of him.

'Can't we get rid of him?' they asked one another. But nobody could think of a way, and the months went on with the ugly little goblin living in the middle of the village, frightening the children, shouting at the dogs and sending all the older folk hurrying home when he began to mutter spells that brought the thunder, or great gales that blew away their chimneys.

At last the folk of Ten O'Clock spoke to the pixie Tiptap who lived in a cave on the nearby hill. He was supposed to be very wise and very good. The little folk told him their trouble and he promised to do what he could for them. 'I will think it over,' he said, 'and I will send you my plan when I have finished it.'

So Ten O'Clock Village waited in patience. At last the plan came, and the head man of the village called a meeting and read out the letter.

Dear friends,

Here is my plan. Prepare a birthday party for the great Wizard Hollabolla-Boo. Say it is for his hundredth birthday and have a cake made with ninety-nine little candles on it and one bigger one in the middle. Invite Fee-Fie-Fo to the party. That is all. Leave the rest to me.

Tiptap

So the little folk obeyed and sent out invitations for Hollabolla-Boo's hundredth birthday, though they had no idea at all who the great wizard was and, indeed, had never even heard of him before!

One of the invitations went to Fee-Fie-Fo, and he wondered who in the world Hollabolla-Boo was. He must really go and see! He would show the hundred-year-old wizard that he, Fee-Fie-Fo, knew even more magic than a wizard! Ho, ho!

A big birthday cake was made by Dame Biscuit, the baker's wife, and Mr Tallow, the candle-man, put eleven rows of nine differently coloured candles on the cake, with a bigger blue candle in the middle.

The great day came. All the folk of the village went

to the little hall where they had their meetings and their parties. There was an enormous table there, and in the middle was the cake. Around it were other plates of cakes and buns, and big mugs of milk.

Would Hollabolla-Boo be there? Yes, he was! He sat at the head of the table, a small figure dressed in a flowing black cloak and pointed hat, with a long white beard. The little folk bowed to him and took their places. Last of all Fee-Fie-Fo came stalking in.

'Ho, so you're Hollabolla-Boo!' he said rudely to the wizard. 'I suppose you think because you are a hundred years old that you are the cleverest person in the world, but you don't know me – Fee-Fie-Fo, the mighty goblin! I can do more magic than anyone in the kingdom.'

'Sit down, Fee-Fie-Fo,' said the wizard in a stern voice. 'This is a party, not a fight. After tea, if you wish, we will see who is the cleverer, you or I!'

'Ha, I'll show you all a few things!' said Fee-Fie-Fo, glaring round in such a terrible way that everyone trembled and shook. He sat down and began his tea, muttering to himself and sticking his sharp elbows into the frightened gnomes next to him.

Nobody took any notice of Fee-Fie-Fo and soon he began to feel angry. His hair stood up straight on his head and sparks flew out of his eyes. He suddenly banged on the table and said, 'Cakes, come to me!'

He opened his mouth, and to the little folk's surprise and anger every single cake on the table flew into his wide mouth.

'What do you think of *that*?' said Fee-Fie-Fo, pleased to see everyone's amazement. 'Now look at this!'

He suddenly turned into a big brown bear and everyone scattered in fright – all except the wizard, who sat still at the table watching him. The goblin changed back to himself again, grinning. He clapped his hands and a fire sprang up from the floor, with green and blue flames that whistled like the wind. It was very strange to see.

'Well, wizard!' said Fee-Fie-Fo rudely. 'Do you think you can better me in magic? I can change myself into anything in the world – a chair...' And he changed into a chair in a trice, and then back again. 'A cat...' And he turned into a black cat with white whiskers, and then back again. 'And even a thunderstorm!' At once he disappeared and a fearful thunderstorm raged for a few minutes round the little hall. Everyone screamed.

When the goblin was back again the wizard spoke, very slowly and mockingly.

'You do no more than a twenty-year-old wizard can do,' he said to the surprised goblin. 'You can change into many things, but you cannot remain anything for more than one minute at a time.'

'That is not true!' cried the goblin at once. 'Tell me anything in the world to change into and I will do so and remain that thing for twenty minutes!'

'And suppose you become yourself again before the twenty minutes is up?' asked the wizard.

'Then I will go away and never come back, for I should be ashamed,' said the goblin, laughing.

'Then change into that middle candle on the birthday cake,' said the wizard.

'Easy!' cried the goblin and disappeared. The middle candle shook a little and a voice came from it. 'I will be in this candle for twenty minutes. Time me by the clock.'

The wizard took out a matchbox and struck a match. 'There is no need to time you by a clock,' he said. 'This candle will burn for twenty minutes, goblin.' He lit the candle and everyone solemnly watched it burning.

It slowly grew smaller as it burnt away. The goblin kept calling out rude things – but suddenly a strange fear fell on him. Suppose he burnt entirely away? If he did, he would not be able to go back to his goblin shape, for he would be gone with the candle.

'I am coming back!' he cried, when the candle had nearly burnt away.

'No, for the twenty minutes is not gone,' cried everyone. 'Oho, goblin, you are not so clever as you thought you were!'

'Well, I will NOT be burnt right away!' said the goblin's voice, and the candle shook on the cake. 'I am too clever for that!'

The candle fell over and the goblin suddenly appeared again. The wizard pointed at him. 'You could not do what you said you could,' he said slowly. 'You must keep your word and go right away!'

'It's a trick, a trick!' shouted the goblin in a rage.

'Ah, the wizard is cleverer than you!' shouted everyone in delight. 'He has tricked you. Go away, goblin, before he tricks you again!'

The goblin gave a mournful howl, leapt up the big chimney and disappeared. That was the end of him. The wizard dragged off his long beard, threw off his cloak and danced a merry jig round the room.

'It's Tiptap the pixie!' cried all the little folk and cheered him till they were hoarse. Then they all went out to get some more cakes, and had a really splendid party.

As for Fee-Fie-Fo, it is said he sometimes howls in the wind. When you hear him you must think of how easily Tiptap tricked him at that party long ago!

Dan's Magic Gold

Dan's Magic Gold

THERE WAS great excitement in Fairyland, for it would soon be the queen's birthday, and that was a very grand day indeed. There was going to be a great party and a great banquet, to which all the fairies, big and little, were invited.

It was the custom to give the fairy queen all sorts of presents on her birthday, for everyone loved her. Some of the fairies were making wonderful necklaces of dewdrops for her, some were weaving beautiful dresses from the rainbow colours to give her, and many were busy putting the scents of lilies and roses into dear little scent bottles for the queen to use.

Now there was one little fairy called Dan, who lived far away on the borders of Fairyland, who did not know what to give the queen. He was not clever with his fingers, and directly he tried to make dresses or necklaces he was so clumsy that all his work was spoilt.

'Oh, dear, oh, dear,' he sighed, again and again, 'I can't make anything for the dear fairy queen. Nothing goes right. What *can* I do?'

He thought he would try weaving a fine curtain of cobwebs for a present, but along came a clumsy old bumblebee and spoilt it all by flying straight into it.

Then he tried stuffing sky-blue cushions with soft downy clouds, but, because he didn't sew them up properly, all the clouds floated out again, and left the cushions flat and hard.

'It's only two days before the queen's birthday,' said the little fairy in despair, 'whatever *shall* I do! I *must* get something really pretty and nice.'

He thought and thought, and asked all his best

friends for their help, but not another idea did he get. The rabbits and birds did their best to help him, but it was all no use.

'Well,' said a grey rabbit at last. 'If you can't think of anything else to make, why not give her something of your own that you have already?'

Dan thought for a minute. Then he said sadly, 'I haven't anything really nice of my own at all. The only valuable thing I've got is a pot of magic gold that I found under a poplar tree once.'

'Why don't you give the queen that?' asked the white owl.

'Because she has so much gold of her own that she won't want any more,' answered the little fairy.

The next day Dan thought he would *have* to take his pot of magic gold to the fairy queen, for he had nothing else at all to give her. So he set off sadly, holding the pot carefully under his arm, and hurrying, because it would take him all day to reach the fairy queen's palace. It was her birthday on the morrow, and he wanted to be there in good time, so that he could give her his present when all the other fairies did.

As he went along he heard a sound of moaning, and stopped. He looked about, and found a hedgehog with one of its legs caught in a prickly bramble. He put down his pot, and after a long time at last freed the hedgehog.

'Oh, thank you,' said the hedgehog gratefully. 'I should have been here all day if you hadn't helped me.'

On went Dan again, hurrying, for he had lost time. He was suddenly stopped by a little white rabbit, who held up his paw and said, 'Oh, please, Dan, will you get this thorn out of my paw; it does hurt so?'

Dan put down his pot again, and spent a long time finding the thorn. At length he pulled it out, and the little rabbit was very grateful.

Poor Dan ran all the way after that, for it was beginning to get very dark, and he did so want to reach the palace in time. He was quite in despair when he suddenly found he had lost his way and didn't know where he was!

He wandered into a bare grass field, where there was not a single flower, and as he went he tripped over a stone and fell forward on his face. His pot was broken, and all the little gold pieces rolled all over the field and sank down into crevices and cracks.

Dan felt too tired and unhappy to get up again, so he just lay there and sobbed himself to sleep, thinking that, after all, he had brought no present for the fairy queen.

On her birthday the queen awoke early, and went out into the garden. She went through the garden gate talking to the king.

'I do wish,' he was saying, 'that we could get some flowers to grow in that horrid bare field of ours. It quite spoils the view.'

'Good gracious,' exclaimed the queen, 'just *look* at the field! Whatever has happened to it in the night?

And look, there's a little fairy asleep there!'

Dan awoke on hearing their voices, and sat up. Imagine his astonishment to find all round him a carpet of bright golden flowers, nodding and dancing in the breeze, and as yellow as sunshine itself!

'Why, it's my magic gold that has grown in the night!' he said in delight. 'And, dear me, I was quite near to the palace after all!'

When he saw the fairy queen and king coming he got up and bowed very low.

'Oh, Dan!' said the queen in a pleased tone. 'What a lovely birthday present you have given me! I always wanted some flowers to grow in this bare field, and now I've got some. Such lovely ones too. Thank you very much indeed!' And she kissed the delighted little fairy.

And that is how the dandelions first came, although in Fairyland everyone calls them 'Dan's gold'.

The Fool and the Magician

The Fool and the Magician

ONCE UPON a time there was an Irish king called Dru. His queen was very beautiful and their baby son was the sturdiest child in the kingdom. They were proud of him and loved him very much.

King Dru had no enemies save one. This was a magician called Yanni, who hated the king because Dru's soldiers had hunted him out of the kingdom. He waited his time, and then when no one was nearby he stole the baby prince from his cot and took him away to his cloudy mountain home far to the north.

What a to-do there was when it was found that the little prince had disappeared! The hunting and searching that went on! It was enough to turn the queen's hair grey.

'It is Yanni who has taken our son,' she wept. 'Only he could have stolen him away so deftly, so surely, without leaving a trace. Send word to him, Dru, and ask what ransom he demands.'

So King Dru sent messengers to the magician. They sought for the great castle in the northern mountains, and at last came to the gates. Yanni was waiting for them, a scornful smile on his face.

'Yes, I stole the prince,' he said. 'I shall keep him and make him my servant. It is fitting that the son of him who drove me away should wait upon me and serve me. It is my revenge.'

'Will you take gold for a ransom?' asked the messengers.

'I am so rich that I have no need of gold,' answered the magician.

'Will you take rare and precious books, the king's ancient jewels or a thousand of his soldiers?'

asked the messengers.

'I have books rarer than any in the world, jewels older than the mountains we stand upon, and at a word can bring ten thousand soldiers round me,' answered the magician scornfully.

'Then is there any way by which we may get back our prince?' asked the messengers in despair.

Yanni thought for a moment, and then he answered sneeringly, 'You shall have back the little prince if your king can answer three questions I set him. He is dull-witted, your sovereign, and his people shall see how stupid he is, compared with Yanni, the great magician.'

'Tell us the three questions, and we will return to King Dru,' said the messengers impatiently.

'Listen,' said Yanno slowly. 'Here is the first – what bridge is there that no man has ever crossed? The second – show me an animal that has never seen the light. The third – what are my thoughts?'

The messengers stood in silence. Surely these

questions were unanswerable by anyone, save magicians? Then they bowed, mounted their horses and rode off to their own country.

King Dru turned pale when he heard the three questions. The two first he perhaps might answer by sending out his servants all over the world – but the third seemed impossible.

Then, far and near, his servants went riding, searching for a bridge that had never yet been crossed and an animal that had never seen the light. But alas, all bridges seem to have been crossed, and not a single animal could they find that lived too far underground to see the light.

When the servants came back from their quest and told the king that nowhere in the world was there a bridge that had not been crossed or an animal that had never seen the light, he was in despair. He called a meeting of his wisest men, but even they could not help him.

The queen had no faith in wise men. She called in Zany, the court fool. He was paid to be funny, and though most people thought that only foolish men could be funny, the queen knew that it took a clever man to make people laugh as Zany did. She had seen something in Zany's eyes that told her he was wiser than most people.

Zany listened to her when she begged his help. For once he made no jokes and played no tricks.

'Can you help me, Zany?' asked the queen. 'Can you answer those three questions?'

'Your Majesty, I can answer all three,' said Zany. 'Send me to the magician and I will bring back with me your little son. Only one thing I ask – and that is that you will allow me to travel in the king's clothes and on his own horse.'

'You shall do anything!' cried the queen gladly. She called the king, and he laughed scornfully when he heard what Zany had said.

'A fool is no match for a wise man,' he said. 'It is a

fool's trick to take my robe and my horse – he will lose his conceited head when Yanni sees through him. But let him do what he wants if it pleases you.'

So Zany, the court fool, dressed himself in the king's purple cloak and placed on his head the golden crown. He mounted the king's own white horse and, with the king behind him followed by a thousand soldiers, he set off towards the north. On his saddle in front of him he carried a little basket, but no one knew what was in it.

At last he stood in front of Yanni the magician, who was too scornful even to rise from his seat. 'So you have come, oh, king,' he said. 'You would set your wits to match mine. Come now, do you know the answers to my three questions? Tell me of the bridge that no man has ever crossed.'

'Even a fool could answer that,' said Zany. 'Has any man ever crossed the bridge of your nose, Yanni? Then that is the bridge I give you in answer!'

'It is a foolish answer, but I will take it,' said Yanni

after a pause, being quite unable to think of any reason why he should not accept the answer. 'But now, the second question – show me an animal whose eyes have never seen the light? What strange creature have you brought me to see?'

'Simply this,' answered the fool quickly, and he put down the basket he had brought with him. Out of it he lifted a tiny kitten, only five days old. The mother cat jumped out of the basket with a mew and licked the tiny creature. 'This kitten has never yet seen the light,' said Zany. 'Its eyes will not open till the twelfth day!'

'A clever answer,' said the magician. 'You are not so dull-witted as I thought you, King Dru. But now comes the hardest question of all – one that surely no one on this earth can answer! What do I think at this very minute?'

'Oh, Yanni,' replied Zany, looking deeply into the magician's strange eyes, 'I know what you are thinking – you think that I am King Dru. But I am not. I am only Zany, the court fool! Have I not read your thoughts right?'

With a loud cry the magician leapt to his feet. He had been tricked. The three questions had been answered. With a thunderous noise the castle suddenly dissolved away, and the magician disappeared. Only one thing was to be seen there – the baby prince sitting bewildered in a high carved chair!

With joy the real King Dru rushed to him, and the thousand soldiers raised their swords in salute. Then home they all went again in triumph, the fool capering at the head in the way he always did.

The Midnight Elves

The Midnight Elves

THERE WAS once a poor tailor who had hardly any work to do. He had a wife and four little children, and though he was willing to work all day long, he could not get enough work to fill even two hours. His children went hungry, and his poor wife wept to see them asking for bread.

One night the tailor went to bed more unhappy than ever before. He had had no work at all that day, and could not give his wife even a penny to buy bread. He tossed and turned in his hard bed, and did not get a wink of sleep.

He heard the clock strike twelve, and after that he

heard something else. It sounded like a scraping and scratching at the windowpane.

Whatever can it be? wondered the tailor. *Is it a cat trying to get in?*

The scraping and scratching went on. Soon the tailor got up and opened the window. Outside stood a company of tiny elves, all dressed in bright green. The moon shone down on them and lit up their tiny faces.

'Are you Snips the tailor?' asked the foremost one.

'Yes,' said Snips, greatly wondering.

'Have you still got that roll of blue cloth you had yesterday?' asked the elf eagerly. 'I saw it when I peeped into your window.'

'Yes,' said Snips again. 'Why do you ask?'

'We are in a great fix,' said the elf, 'and we wondered if you would help us. Our master, the prince of Dreamland, is holding a ball at dawn today, and has commanded us to appear before him at cockcrow wearing blue suits to match his new carriage. Alas! We have made a mistake, as you see, and are all in green! We dare not appear before the prince like this, and not knowing what else to do, we have come to you!'

'You want me to make suits for all of you before dawn?' said the tailor in amazement. 'But I have never made clothes for such little folks before – I should not know how to!'

'Yes, you would,' answered the elf. 'We have often seen you making clothes for your children's dolls. We are much the same size. Oh, we beg of you, grant us our wish, and you will never regret it.'

The little creature spoke so earnestly that the tailor could not help granting his request. He bade them come in, and then he led the way to his workroom. He took down the roll of fine blue cloth, and began to cut it into strips. There were ten of the little folk, and the tailor reckoned he had just enough stuff. He was sad to cut up his beautiful cloth, for it was the only thing he had left to sell.

As he was busy fitting the cloth to the tiny elves his wife came gliding into the room. She had missed him from their bed, and had come to seek him. She stared in astonishment to see the little company of elves standing on the work table.

Her husband told her what had happened, and she listened in surprise.

'I will sew on the buttons and make the buttonholes,' she said, 'then the suits will certainly be ready in time.'

All night long the tailor and his wife worked hard. Fifteen minutes before cockcrow ten little blue suits lay ready on the table.

The elves quickly put them on, did up all the buttons and shouted in joy to see how nicely the suits fitted them.

'Thank you a thousand times!' they cried, and off they flew to attend their master, the prince of Dreamland. The tailor and his wife were very tired, and putting their heads down upon the table, they slept.

When the sun was up, and all the children were awake and crying for something to eat, they awoke. They looked around the workroom, and remembered how they had spent their night. Snips arose, and taking up the few pieces of blue cloth still left, he went to put them away in the cupboard.

But what a surprise when he opened the door! Inside the cupboard were bales upon bales of magnificent cloth. There was cloth of silver and cloth of gold. There was a bale of rainbow-hued silk, such as the tailor had never seen in his life before! There was also a pile of rich cloth all embroidered with flashing gems.

'Look!' cried Snips in amazement. 'Where did this come from?'

'From the elves!' said his wife in delight. 'This is their return for your kindness to them last night! Oh, Snips, put some of this stuff in the window! You will soon have all the work you want, for there is not another tailor in the kingdom who has such beautiful cloths as these!'

So Snips put the cloth in the window, and soon customers came pouring in. Never had they seen such beautiful stuffs before, and everyone wanted a dress made of this, or a coat made of that.

Then who should come by in his carriage, but the king of that country himself! When he saw the tailor's window he stopped in surprise. His eye caught sight of the gem-studded cloth, and he jumped out of the carriage eagerly.

'Ho, tailor!' he said. 'You shall make me my new cloak of that stuff in your window! Here is a purse of gold in payment for the cloth. You shall have another when the cloak is finished.'

How excited the tailor and his family were! How Snips worked and worked! But no matter how much of his lovely new cloths he used, the cupboard was always full.

One day Snips was so rich that he left his tiny cottage and went to a fine house in the middle of the town. He took with him the old cupboard, and folks laughed at him.

'What does he want with that old thing?' they said to one another. 'He might well have left that behind!'

But Snips knew better. He was not going to leave his good luck behind him. Never again did he hear of the ten elves, though for many years he kept the little green suits they had left behind in case they returned again for them.

But they never did, so now his grandchildren use them for their dolls. They always have to put the little suits away very carefully after playing with them, for as Snips their grandfather says, 'You never know when the elves might ask for them back!'

One Bonfire Night

One Bonfire Night

THE LITTLE folk in the village of Tick-Tack were most excited. For the first time in their lives they were going to have fireworks on Bonfire Night!

'Imagine it – fireworks!' said Cheery-One. 'Rockets that fly up to the clouds and then burst into little stars!'

'Squibs that will jump round Old Man Grumpy's feet,' said Tricky.

'Wheels of fire that go round and round spitting flames all the time!' said Jinky.

'What fun we'll have!' said Tippy. 'And, oh, the noise! The lovely BANGS! The big WHOOSHES!

The splutterings and sizzlings and cracklings!'

'We'll have to remember to keep our dogs indoors,' said Cheery-One. 'My little dog doesn't like bangs. He'd go mad with fright if I left him outside.'

'The same with my cat,' said Jinky. 'She hates even a spark to jump out of the fire. I simply don't know *what* she'd do if a rocket went off near her. I shall keep her indoors and tell her to look for mice.'

'And I'll get my pony Whitefoot out of the field, and put him into a shed,' said Tippy. 'I wouldn't want him to gallop away and never come back!'

'Don't you think we ought to send out the bellman with his bell, to warn everyone in the village to keep their animals indoors on Bonfire Night?' said Cheery-One anxiously. 'You see, we've never had fireworks before, and people might not think of their cats and dogs and ponies.'

'Yes. I'll go and see the bellman,' said Jinky. 'And we'll put a big notice up on the wall too.'

Away he went, and soon the bellman was walking

through the village, ringing his bell loudly. Then, when people ran round him to see what was the matter, he stood still and shouted in his biggest, deepest voice.

'Hear what I say, people of Tick-Tack Village. On Tuesday night, there will be a grand firework display, with bangs and crashes, flames and fire. Keep your animals indoors for kindness' sake on Bonfire Night.'

A big notice was put up on a wall too, and everyone read it. Old Witch Green-Eyes heard the bellman's bell ringing as he went up and down the village, and she looked crossly out of her window.

'Stop that noise!' she cried. 'I'm making a powerful spell, with Cinders, my black cat, and you're upsetting it. The magic won't come. Stop that noise, I say!'

But the bellman didn't stop, and he went on shouting out his message at the top of his voice.

'What's that he says? Keep our cats and dogs in on Tuesday night?' said Witch Green-Eyes. 'Just because of fireworks! I never heard of such a silly idea in my life! Pampering our animals like that! Shutting them up – putting them in closed rooms! What are we coming to, fussing about animals, as if they couldn't look after themselves! *I* shan't do anything of the sort. My cat Cinders can look after herself perfectly well. All this fuss and bother!'

'You'd better keep your cat indoors, all the same,' said Tricky, who was nearby. 'Cinders is a good little worker for you, and helps you with all kinds of magic spells. Out of kindness you should keep her from the bangs and crashes and whooshes and flashes.'

'I'll turn you into a cat yourself if you dare to tell me what to do!' said the witch, and that made Tricky run off at top speed.

Well, when Bonfire Night came the cats and the dogs of Tick-Tack Village were most surprised to find that they were taken indoors. Dogs were taken out of their kennels, Whitefoot the pony was led from his field to a shed, cats were called indoors and made comfortable by the fire or told to listen for mice.

But old Witch Green-Eyes wasn't going to fuss over Cinders, *her* cat! When Cinders ran out into the garden just as it got dark she shut the door on her as usual.

So when the fireworks began Cinders was out all alone in the dark, sitting patiently beside a rathole.

CRASH! That was a firework exploding, the first one of all. Cinders almost jumped out of her skin.

BANG-BANG-WHOOOOOOOOSH! That was a very big rocket set off by Tricky, three gardens away. Cinders tried her hardest to squeeze down the rathole, shaking with fright.

Sizzle-crackle-BONG-BONG! Goodness knows what that was – but the noise and the sudden glare so terrified poor Cinders that she gave a great yowl, leapt over the wall and disappeared down the road at sixty miles an hour.

And when Bonfire Night was over, and all the fireworks were finished, old Witch Green-Eyes opened her window, calling to Cinders as usual.

'Cinders, Cinders! Come along in to the nice warm fire! I want you to help me with a new spell.'

But no Cinders came leaping up to the windowsill. No big black cat came purring to Witch Green-Eyes to help her with the strange new spell.

Cinders was miles away, still terrified, trembling from head to feet, her bright green eyes staring in fright. Her feet were sore with running for miles, and she was hungry, thirsty and so tired that at last she fell down on a doorstep and could not move.

And there she was found by a small girl called Alice, who loved all animals, but had no pet of her own. Alice carried Cinders indoors, and petted her and gave her some warm milk. Her mother stared at the cat in surprise.

'What a fine cat! And what wonderful bright green eyes! Anyone would have said she was a witch's cat, to look at her. Poor thing – whoever owned her should have shut her indoors on Bonfire Night.'

'I want her,' said Alice. 'If she doesn't go back

home, I want her, Mother. She's a wonderful cat. I'm sure she knows magic!'

Cinders didn't mean to go back to Tick-Tack Village. She remembered the bangs and crashes and glares, and she trembled. She loved kind little Alice. She liked not having to work so hard at magic spells, and soon forgot most of them.

But she didn't forget one special bit of magic. Cinders knew a good-luck spell, and whenever Alice was feeling sad and needed cheering up, Cinders disappeared into the garden, and there, behind some bushes, she made a small good-luck spell for the little girl.

No wonder Alice said that black cats were lucky. Cinders certainly brought plenty of luck for *her*! And when the next Bonfire Night came Cinders didn't mind a bit. She lay cuddled warmly on Alice's lap, and was stroked and petted. Who cared about bangs and crashes outdoors then? Not Cinders!

As for old Witch Green-Eyes, she missed her black

cat terribly, because now she couldn't make half the magic she needed. But nobody was sorry for her. *I'm* not either. She should have looked after Cinders on Bonfire Night, just as you and I look after *our* pets – don't you think so?

The Wind's Party

The Wind's Party

'I WANT to blow hard!' said the autumn wind. 'I want to rush around and sweep things away in front of me. I haven't had a good blow for ages.'

'Well, blow then,' said a little cloud. 'I think I shall rather like it if you do!'

'I don't want to waste all my breath on a small thing like you!' said the wind. 'I want to blow hundreds and thousands of things away. I want to have some real fun.'

'Well, have a party, and ask the trees to come to it!' said the little cloud. 'Tell them to put on party dresses of all colours – and then blow as hard as you can! You'll have such fun blowing off their red, yellow, orange and brown leaves!'

'That's a good idea!' said the wind. 'I could blow the leaves high in the air, and all round about – and then I could puff them along the ground, and sweep them into the ditches. I think I could really have some fun doing that.'

So the wind went round about whispering in among all the trees. 'Come to a party, all of you! Come to a party! Put on your prettiest colours, and come to the wind's party!'

The beech put on a dress of brightest gold and shimmered in the sunshine. The hazel put on pale gold and so did the silver birch.

The chestnut put on orange and yellow, and the wild cherry put on the brightest pink. The oak turned a russet brown, and the creeper on the houses nearby flamed into crimson.

'Fine, fine!' cried the wind, as he swept round. 'Are you ready for the party! It's a party for your leaves, you know. I want them to play with, I want to make them dance and twist in the air. Are you ready?'

Then, with a rush, the wind swept through the trees. The frost had touched them the night before, and they were loose. The wind pulled them off.

Then off into the air went the coloured leaves, red, yellow, pink and brown, whirling and twirling, swaying and falling.

What a game the wind had with them! How he blew them about, and made them dance and prance! Soon the trees were bare, for their coloured party frocks were gone!

'Come and play too!' cried the autumn wind to the children. 'Come along, come along! For every leaf you catch before it reaches the ground you shall have a happy day next year!'

Let's go and catch them as they whirl in the air. Let's see if we can catch three hundred and sixty-five, a whole year of wonderful, happy days!

We're coming to your party too, autumn wind. Please wait for us, do!

The Brownie Who
Thought He Was
Clever

The Brownie Who Thought He Was Clever

ONCE THERE was a little brownie called Bron who was hunting for lost treasure. He knew a pot of gold was hidden on Rainbow Hill, but he didn't know how to get there. So he went to the Simple Witch, and asked her the way.

'Go down that path,' she said. 'It leads to hilly country. Cross as many hills as there are legs on a spider, and you will find a river. Row down the river for as many miles as there are legs on a butterfly. After that count as many oak trees as there are petals on a wild rose. Climb the last one, and you will see a hill where, if you dig, you will find your pot of gold.'

Bron thought her directions rather strange, but he wrote them all down. He said goodbye and went away, humming cheerfully, thinking he would soon find the gold.

Now, Bron was a nice little brownie but, like a good many people, he thought he knew everything. For one thing, he felt sure he knew how many legs a spider had.

'I can't think why the Simple Witch didn't say cross six hills, instead of "as many hills as there are legs on a spider",' he said to himself. 'I suppose she thought it sounded clever! Anyway, they aren't very big hills. I'll soon be there.'

When he had crossed six hills he stopped and looked for the river. There wasn't a sign of one anywhere! 'The witch was wrong!' said Bron angrily, and ran all the way back to tell her so. But she laughed at him.

'It's you who are wrong,' she said, and wouldn't say another word.

At that moment, a spider dropped down from the roof and swung just above Bron's nose. And oh, dear me! Bron saw it had eight legs, not six. So he ought to have crossed eight hills. He did feel silly! He had felt so certain that spiders had six legs. He slipped quietly out of the witch's cottage.

Over the hills he went again, one, two, three, four, fix, six, seven, eight. Then he looked around.

And there was the shining river! He ran down to it, and jumped into a boat. 'I'm to row as many miles as the legs on a butterfly,' he said. 'Aha, Simple Witch, you won't catch me this time! A spider has eight legs, so a butterfly has eight too! That's eight miles I must row!'

He set off. It was a long way, and the eight miles seemed more like sixteen. His arms ached and his head was hot with the sun. But at last he had rowed eight miles, and he looked around for the oak trees. But there weren't any!

Is the witch wrong or am I? thought Bron. *I'd better*

catch a butterfly and count its legs! At that moment a white butterfly perched on Bron's boat, and he leapt forward to count its legs.

'Six!' he cried. 'Six! And I've rowed eight miles. Oh, dear! Why didn't I count a butterfly's legs first? I thought for sure they would have the same amount as a spider. Now I've got to go back two miles, and I'm so tired!' Back he rowed for two miles, and sure enough, there were the oak trees.

'Now I've got to count as many trees as there are petals on a wild rose,' said Bron. 'I'm going to pick a wild rose and see how many petals it has first!'

He jumped out of his boat and went to a wild rose bush. He picked the first rose he saw, counted its petals and stuck it into his buttonhole.

'Four!' he cried. 'Now I'll count four trees and climb the last one. Then I'll see the hill where the gold is hidden!' So he counted four trees and climbed the last. But there was no hill to be seen! Not a sign of one! Bron was very angry indeed.

'I counted the petals!' he cried. 'So the horrid witch is wrong! I'll go back and tell her so!'

He rowed back for six miles, and crossed the eight hills. Then up the path he went, and burst into the witch's cottage. She was talking to another brownie, and was telling him the way to go to find the hidden gold.

'It's no good going!' stormed Bron. 'I've been, and it's all wrong! The witch doesn't know.' The witch smiled and said nothing.

'Well, I'll see for myself,' said the other brownie, catching a spider and counting its legs. 'I'll come back tomorrow and tell you how I got on. Goodbye!'

'I'll come back tomorrow too!' said Bron to the witch. 'And perhaps you'll admit you are wrong when we both tell you!'

As he went home, his wild rose petals began to fall – one, two, three, four.

The next day Bron went to the witch's cottage. There was no sign of the other brownie.

'Aha!' said Bron. 'Your directions were as wrong for him as for me! He can climb the tree and look for as long as he likes, but he won't see a hill anywhere!'

The old witch stirred her pot and said nothing. Presently she lifted her head and listened. Bron listened too. Yes, someone was coming. Who could it be? Perhaps it was the other brownie coming back to say he had been given the wrong directions too. The footsteps came nearer, and then Bron saw that it *was* the other brownie.

And he had got a pot of gold!

'Where did you get that from?' asked Bron in astonishment.

'From the Rainbow Hill, of course,' said the brownie. 'I crossed eight hills, rowed six miles, climbed the fifth oak tree, and from there saw the top of the hill away in the distance. The rest was easy.'

'Climbed the fifth tree!' said Bron. 'But I climbed the fourth! Wild roses have four petals, not five, and the witch said, "Count as many trees as there are petals on a wild rose," didn't she?'

'Yes,' said the brownie, laughing. 'But you must have counted the petals of a rose that was nearly over! The petals fall one by one, you know, silly! Dear me, and I thought you were so clever, Bron! Fancy not counting the petals of two or three wild roses, to make sure of the right number!'

Bron remembered how his petals had fallen as he went home, and he blushed red and looked at the Simple Witch.

'I beg your pardon,' he said. 'You were right, and I was wrong. I'm not as clever as I thought I was!'

'Nobody ever is,' said the Simple Witch, and wouldn't say another word. And what I'd like to know is this: would you have found the pot of gold or wouldn't you? I wonder!

Peronel and His Pot of Glue

Peronel and His Pot of Glue

ONCE UPON a time, long, long ago, the king of Fairyland sat at dinner. He had a wonderful old dish in front of him, full of fairy cakes. He was very fond of that dish, for no one knew how old it was, and it was certainly a most convenient dish to have, for whatever you wanted to eat, you had only to tap the dish seven times and say what you wanted . . . when, lo and behold, there it was on the dish in front of you!

The king found it very useful indeed for parties, for if the cook suddenly found he hadn't enough food for everyone, he simply borrowed the old dish and told it what he wanted.

When the king had eaten two fairy cakes at the end of his dinner he rang the bell for the table to be cleared. The fairy pages bustled up, and started carrying off all the things. One of them, a new one, was very nervous.

'Be careful of that old dish,' said the king to him.

'Yes, Your Majesty,' answered the page. But, alas! The king's cat suddenly ran against his legs; down went the page, and CRASH went the dish into three large pieces!

'Oh, dear! Oh, dear!' said all the fairy attendants.

'Oh, dear! Oh, dear!' said the king sadly.

'Oh, dear! Oh, dear!' wept the pageboy.

'Never mind,' said the king at last, 'we may be able to stick it together again.'

All sorts of fairy paste and fairy glue were brought. The three pieces were carefully fitted together and glued.

'Now, we'll see if it's all right,' said the king cheerfully. He tapped the dish seven times, but just as he was saying what he wanted – crack! – the dish was in pieces again.

The fairies tried again and again to mend it, but it was of no use. When the king tapped it, into three pieces it cracked!

At last the king offered a reward to any fairy who was clever enough to find a glue that would mend his dish properly.

Fairies came from far and near with all sorts of paste and glue, but none of them was any good.

At last there came to the king's court a little dancing fairy called Peronel, with naughty twinkles in his eyes and mischievous dimples in his cheeks. He swung a large pot of sweet-smelling stuff in his hand.

'Your Majesty!' he cried, as he knelt before the king, 'I've found something to stick your dish together. It's the strongest glue in Fairyland!'

'What is it made of?' asked the king.

'Wild rose honey and poppy-stalk milk, catkin dust and honeysuckle juice!' sang Peronel gaily. 'And there's morning frost in it too, and sticky spider's web. There are too many things to tell you, and I stirred it all up with my magic wand.'

'Let's see if it will stick my dish together,' said the king, greatly pleased.

The little fairy quickly glued the three pieces together, and put the dish in the sun to dry. Then the king tapped it seven times, and said, 'I should like some apples.'

Immediately the dish became full of rosy apples!

'Hurrah!' cried the king. 'The dish is mended! You shall have the reward, and stay at my palace for seven days!'

Peronel thanked the king, and went off with his pot of glue. But he was the most mischievous little fairy in all Fairyland. He was so proud of his glue, he couldn't stop gluing everything.

He glued the underneath of the plates so that no one could lift them off the table! He glued the seat of the Lord High Chamberlain's chair, and the poor chamberlain had a terribly hard job to get up again!

Then he went into the kitchen and put glue on all the taps, so that the fairy cooks spent nearly all the morning trying to unstick their hands! He was a very mischievous little fairy indeed. But somehow he was so merry and gay that no one had the heart to scold him very hard.

At last something happened that made the king say that all this mischief *must* be stopped.

The little fairy had spilt some of his glue in the great hall where the king received his visitors, so that when his visitors arrived and walked up the hall they suddenly found themselves unable to stir, for something held their feet firmly to the floor!

The king was angry, and yet he could not help smiling at the mischievous little fairy, who was laughing by the door.

So when the visitors had gone at last, he called a meeting of the fairies to decide what should be done with mischievous little Peronel and his pot of glue.

'Let him do something useful,' said one of his councillors. 'Then he will not need to waste his magic glue on playing tricks.'

'Can anyone advise what work we shall give him?' asked the king.

'Yes, I can,' answered a tree fairy. 'Last year most of the chestnut buds died before they came into leaf, for it was so cold that the frost killed them. If only they were painted with that strong glue, the frost couldn't get through that, and they would be quite safe.'

'That's a good idea!' said the king. 'That shall be your work, little Peronel. You can start straight away now, as it's early spring, and perhaps that will keep you out of mischief.'

So now the little glue fairy is very busy every spring painting the chestnut buds to keep the frost out. And if you touch one, you will feel how very, very sticky his magic glue is!

The Magic Knitting
Needles

The Magic Knitting Needles

MOTHER CLICK-CLACK had a wonderful pair of knitting needles. You should just have seen them!

All she had to do was to set them by a ball of wool and say, 'Click-clack now, needles, let me hear you click-clack!'

And at once those needles would set to work knitting all by themselves. They flew in and out, making a clickity-clackity noise rather like two or three clocks ticking away at once. The ball of wool unwound quickly as the needles pulled at it, and very soon Mother Click-Clack would see a long stocking made, or a baby's bonnet, or a child's jersey.

It was really marvellous.

One day she lent her magic knitting needles to Sally Simple. Sally had got all behind with her knitting, so she was very pleased to have the needles.

'When the needles have made what you want bring them straight back to me,' said Mother Click-Clack. 'Don't leave them about, whatever you do, especially not near wool. Bring them straight back.'

'Very well, Mother Click-Clack,' said Sally. So off she went with the silvery needles, delighted to think her knitting would so soon be done. She fetched a ball of blue wool and three balls of white. She wanted a little coat for her sister's baby.

'Click-clack now, needles,' she said. 'Click-clack, I want a baby's coat.'

The needles set to work at once. They flew in and out, making a fine click-clackety noise. The balls of wool unwound quickly, and lo and behold, Sally Simple saw a baby's blue and white coat being made before her very eyes. It was really marvellous! It didn't take longer than ten minutes to do.

Now, as you know, Sally Simple had promised to take the magic needles straight back to Mother Click-Clack when she had finished with them. But Sally had a bad memory and didn't always do what she said she would.

She didn't take the needles back. No, she so very badly wanted to take the blue and white coat to show her sister that she forgot all about her promise. What did it matter anyway! She would only be about an hour at her sister's.

She put on her hat, took up the dear little coat and ran off. She left the magic needles by themselves on the table – and, do you know, quite near them was Sally's great basket of wools!

There were balls of brown wool for knitting stockings, balls of black wool for socks, balls of blue wool for coats and bonnets, balls of white wool for vests and all kinds of odd balls for things like scarves and mittens.

The magic needles lay quietly for a minute or two. Then they gave a little jump towards the basket of wools. They gave another little jump, and another – and then they landed right into the middle of the basket.

Ah! This is wonderful! The needles had seldom had so much wool to work with. They began to fly in and out merrily. The balls of wool jumped and jerked as the wool unwound from them. Clickety-clackety, clickety-clackety, clickety-clackety went those needles.

Now as the needles hadn't been told what to make, they just made what they thought. The first things they made were two pairs of brown stockings for the legs of the kitchen table.

As soon as the stockings were finished, they flew to the legs of the table and slipped themselves on. My, they did look splendid!

Then the needles began to work with the blue wool – a bonnet for the clock. Fancy that!

The bonnet was soon made. It even had two knitted ribbons to tie it tightly. It flew to the clock and put itself neatly on the top, tying the ribbons in a neat bow. Dear dear! Whatever next!

The needles clickety-clacked at the white wool. Vests for the chairs next. Aha! How warm the chairs would be wearing woollen vests! It didn't take those needles long to make four long white vests. They flew off to the chairs and put themselves on at once. How nice and warm they were!

This time the needles knitted the pink wool and the yellow wool together and made a long scarf for the dog who was lying peacefully by the fire. Wasn't he surprised to find a warm scarf suddenly knotting itself round his neck! He did look smart!

The cat walked into the kitchen at that moment and the needles clicked merrily in the blue wool. They made a blue dress for the cat and a blue bonnet. Puss miaowed in surprise when she found them on her back and head. She did look funny in them! She sat down in her basket and wondered how to get them off.

The magic needles knitted black socks for the stool and a coat for the coal scuttle. They knitted one long stocking for the poker and a petticoat for the lamp. They knitted a pink coat for the grandfather clock, with a pink bonnet to match. The grandfather clock didn't like them. After all, it was a grandfather, not a baby! But it had to wear them.

Then the needles started on a jersey for the piano, with leggings to match. This was a very big job and the needles clicked hard. Clickety-clack, clickety-clack, clickety-clack, clickety-clack they went.

And in the middle of it all, Sally Simple came back.

'Now, where are those knitting needles?' she said. 'I must take them back to Mother Click-Clack.'

Clickety-clack, clickety-clack went the needles busily. Sally Simple stared at her wool basket – there was hardly any wool left. Wherever had it gone?

Then she looked round the room – and oh, how she stared at the sights she saw!

'The dog's got a scarf round his neck! The cat's got a dress and bonnet on!' cried Sally.

'Clickety-clack,' said the busy needles.

'My goodness! The table's got stockings! And the stool has got socks! And the coal scuttle is wearing a coat! Bless us all! Look at that!' cried Sally in dismay. 'Oh, look at the lamp – it's wearing a woollen petticoat! And the grandfather clock has got a pink bonnet and coat! What's this on the poker – mercy me, a stocking! And the chairs have got vests and the clock's got a bonnet! Oh, why did I leave those needles near my wool!'

She went to take them – and at the same moment they finished the jersey and leggings for the piano. They shot to the piano and put themselves on – dear me, how very strange the piano looked!

Sally Simple snatched up the needles and ran off to Mother Click-Clack with them. She was almost in tears.

'Your horrid, horrid needles have knitted up all

my balls of wool!' she said. 'They've made a dress and bonnet for the cat – stockings for the table legs – and . . .'

Mother Click-Clack began to laugh. 'Oh, Sally, you'll be the death of me!' she laughed. 'Fancy letting the needles do all that! Didn't I tell you to bring them back as soon as you'd finished with them? I know their little ways.'

'Now I've got to undo all those silly vests and stockings and socks and bonnets,' cried Sally Simple. 'It will take me ages!'

'Well, I'm sorry, Sally,' said Mother Click-Clack. 'But it's your own fault. You should give back things you've borrowed as soon as ever you can.'

Poor Sally Simple. She's still undoing the jersey and leggings that the needles made for the piano.

The Wicked Witch

The Wicked Witch

ONCE UPON a time, there was a wicked witch who had been sent right away from Fairyland by the fairy queen.

'You must stay away from us for fifty years,' commanded the queen. 'Then if you have learnt to be better, perhaps you may come back.'

'When I come back I'll have my revenge,' growled the old witch. 'I'll come, and I'll carry you away where no one will ever find you.'

For fifty years she stayed away from Fairyland, and never once did she do a good deed, or think a good thought. She made plans to spirit away the fairy queen, and every night she thought and thought how she could manage it.

If only I could make the queen touch my hand, she would be in my power, thought the old witch, *but I know she won't even see me. Still, I'll try.*

So when the fifty years had gone by she sent a polite note to the queen.

Your Majesty,
I am sorry for my evil deeds. Will you see me and give me your forgiveness?

The queen showed the note to the king.

'Pooh, rubbish!' he exclaimed. 'Why, she never ceased to be wicked all these fifty years. She wants to do you some harm. I shall forbid her to see you, my dear.'

The old witch was terribly angry when she got the queen's answer.

'I *will* see her!' she stormed. 'I know what I'll do! I'll

dress up as a grand princess, and drive up in a beautiful carriage! I'll jump out at the door, and when I see the queen coming down the hall to greet me I'll run forward and take her hand! Then as soon as I touch her, she'll be in my power, and I'll spirit her away!'

The witch laid her plans carefully. She sent a grand letter to the queen to say that the princess of Cloudland was coming to see her in three days. Then she prepared a wondrous carriage drawn by twenty coal-black horses. Behind the carriage stood six coal-black footmen, each with a silver trumpet which they were to blow as they went through the queen's gate.

'Now, I'll disguise myself!' chuckled the wicked old witch. She dressed herself in a robe of silver and gold, and she put a lovely wig of golden hair over her own lank grey hairs. She put on a golden headdress, and hung from it a silver veil to hide her wicked old face.

Last of all, she slipped on a pair of high-heeled silver shoes.

On the third day, she started off in her carriage to visit the queen. Her face was covered by her veil, and no one could guess that this golden-haired, silver-shod princess was really and truly the evil old witch.

As the carriage rolled through the gates the footmen blew on their silver trumpets.

Tan-tara! Tan-tan-tara!

The fairy queen heard, and looked from her window.

'Dear me! It's the Princess of Cloudland already! I really must go down and meet her!' she cried, and ran downstairs into the hall.

The old witch jumped out of the carriage and climbed up the steps to the front door. She grinned behind her veil as she saw the fairy queen coming down the hall to meet her. She stepped on the big doormat, and was just going to take the queen's hand when suddenly the high heels of her new silver shoes caught in the thick doormat, and down she fell with a crash.

Off rolled her headdress, and off rolled her veil. Off came her golden wig. And there lay the hideous old witch on the polished floor of the hall.

Up came the king and put his arm round the queen.

'Take the witch away and lock her up!' he cried.

The servants took hold of her and hurried her away.

'I *nearly* got her, I *nearly* got her!' screamed the witch angrily.

'Ah, but you just *didn't*!' said the Lord High Chamberlain, poking her with his long black stick. '*There's many a fall 'twixt the mat and the hall*, you know, and it will pay you to remember *that*, mistress witch!'

Games in Goblin Land

Games in Goblin Land

ALLAN LOVED playing games indoors on a rainy day. He had draughts, snap and beat-your-neighbour-out-of-doors. I expect you know how to play them all, don't you?

But nobody liked playing games with Allan because he always wanted to win – and if he didn't, he either cheated or flew into a temper and wouldn't play any more!

His father was angry with him. 'You must learn to lose, as well as to win!' he often said to Allan. 'You must never cheat, and as for flying into a temper and throwing the cards and the counters about, well!

You ought to be ashamed of yourself!'

Now one day it was wet, and a friend of Allan's mother came to ask if Allan would like to bring his games to her house and play them with Michael, her little boy. So Allan took a basket with his draughtboard and draughtsmen in, and his two packs of cards to play snap and beat-your-neighbour-out-of-doors.

He ran down a little path that went along the side of a field and, as he ran, the box of draughtsmen upset and rolled out of the basket. Allan bent down to pick them up. He found all but one, and this last one he could not find!

He thought it must have gone into the thick hedge that grew by the side of the path, so he crawled into it – and then he had the surprise of his life!

In the shelter of the hedge sat three small goblins, playing a curious game with fans and balls that Allan had never seen before. He stared and stared – and they stared back.

'Come and play,' said one of the goblins. He offered Allan a fan and two balls. The little boy took them in delight and sat down beside the goblins. This was an exciting adventure!

But he couldn't play the game, however much he tried – so he fetched his basket and games, and showed them to the goblins.

'We do not know how to play those games,' they said.

'Oh, they are easy,' said Allan at once, delighted to think that if the goblins did not know how to play the games, he would easily win! 'This game is called draughts. And this one is called snap. And this one, played with these cards, is called beat-your-neighbour-out-of-doors!'

He showed the goblins how to play draughts – and one of them began to play with him. But, you know, goblin brains are sharp – and the little fellow easily beat Allan! The boy lost his temper – and what do you suppose he did? He picked up the draughtboard and threw it hard at the surprised goblin!

There was a silence for a moment. Then the goblin stood up and frowned angrily.

'So that's how you play your game of draughts!' he said. 'I suppose you play your games of snap and beat-your-neighbour-out-of-doors in the same way! Well! Come with us and we will show you how we play those games in our country! We will see if you like that!'

The three goblins caught hold of the bad-tempered little boy and pushed him through the hedge to the other side – and to Allan's enormous astonishment he saw that he was in a small town of little hillocks, in each of which lived a goblin. The three goblins with Allan clapped their hands and called out something. At once the doors in the hillock houses flew open and out came scores of small goblins just like the others, all dressed in grey suits and hats, and all with pointed ears and feet.

'We want to teach this boy a few games,' said one of

the three goblins with a grin. 'It seems to us that he doesn't know how to play the games he has with him. First we would like to teach him how to play draughts!'

'Ho, ho, ho!' laughed all the goblins at once. 'We shall show him!' They stood in a ring and took hands. 'Come into the middle!' they shouted to Allan. 'We will show you how to play our game of draughts!'

Allan was pushed into the middle of the ring. Then the goblins danced round once, and sang a strange, chanting song that went like this:

'North wind blow!
South wind too!
East and west wind
Where are you?'

Immediately there came the four winds, blowing hard from the north, south, east and west. They came right into the ring of dancing goblins, and began to blow poor Allan!

His cap flew off, and his coat flew open. His hair stood up and there was a loud whistling in his ears. He could hardly stand upright, and he felt dreadfully cold.

'This is our game of draughts!' shouted the goblins in glee. 'Isn't it draughty? Do you feel a draught? Do you think you will win? It's no use losing your temper in this game – because the winds won't let you! They do love a game of draughts!'

Allan became so out of breath with the blowing of the four winds that he could not say a single word. He staggered about in the ring of goblins, puffing and blowing, trying to keep his coat on and feeling colder and colder!

As suddenly as they had come, the winds went. The goblins unlinked their hands and laughed at Allan, who sat down to get his breath. He felt giddy.

'Did you like our game of draughts?' asked the goblins. 'Wasn't it fun? Now we'll show you how to play snap!'

They made a ring again, and put Allan in the middle. Then they began to chant another song:

'Here's a chap
Who likes to snap.
Play with him, pup,
And snap him up!'

Then into the ring there ran a big puppy dog, full of fun and nonsense. When he saw Allan he ran at him and snapped playfully at the little boy's legs.

'Don't, don't!' shouted Allan. 'Go away! I don't want to play with you, you nasty little puppy. Go away!'

He flapped his handkerchief at the puppy, and it woofed joyfully. It snapped at the handkerchief and tore it in half. Allan became very angry.

'Look what you've done!' he cried. 'You've spoilt my handkerchief. Go away!'

The goblins shrieked with laughter to see the puppy playing snap with Allan. The little boy took his cap and tried to smack the puppy with it. But the dog snapped at it eagerly, snatched it right out of Allan's hand and ran off round the ring with it!

'He's snapped the cap, he's snapped the cap!' yelled the goblins. 'Oh, doesn't he play snap well? Do you like the way we play snap here, Allan?'

The puppy shook the cap and bit it hard. Then he ran at Allan again and began to snap at his coat. The small boy was almost in tears, for, although he could see that the puppy would not hurt him, he was very angry to have to play such a strange, silly game of snap!

The puppy jumped up and snapped a button of Allan's coat. The goblins cheered him and then sent him out of the ring. Allan picked up his torn handkerchief and his bitten cap and button.

'Well, the puppy won that game!' said the goblins. 'Now for a game of beat-your-neighbour-out-of-doors!'

They took Allan to a small hillock house and pushed him inside. They shut the door. He was left alone for a minute or two, and then the door suddenly burst open. In came a small goblin pretending to be very angry. He waved a stick at Allan and shouted, 'Get out of my house or I will beat you out!' Allan rushed out at once and the goblin chased after him. Seeing the next house with the door standing open, Allan rushed inside and banged the door. But, dear me, there was a goblin in there, and he had a stick too!

He jumped up and shouted, 'Get out of my house or I will beat you out!' Allan gave a shout and rushed out again, with the goblin after him, waving his stick. In and out of the hillock houses they rushed, and at last Allan ran into an open door again, for he could see there was no goblin inside. He banged the door and bolted it. Then he sat down to get his breath.

They can't get me out of here! he thought to himself. But he was mistaken, for there came a rumbling in the chimney – and down came a goblin, almost dropping on top of Allan, who had bent down to see what the noise was.

'Get out of my house or I will beat you out!' shouted

the goblin gleefully, waving his stick. Allan unbolted the door in a hurry and rushed outside.

All the other goblins stood there, grinning and shouting in great delight.

'Do you like the way we play beat-your-neighbour-out-of-doors?' they cried. 'Shall we teach you another game? We have a fine one called put-me-in-a-coal-hole!'

Allan thought that didn't sound at all a nice game, so he shook his head.

'No, thank you,' he said. 'Please let me go to my friend's. He is expecting me. I am sorry I lost my temper when I played draughts with you in the hedge. I like my way of playing our games best. I don't like yours at all.'

'Well, if you had played your game properly without losing your temper, we wouldn't have shown you how we could play!' said one of the goblins. 'You can go on your way. We don't expect to ever see you here again – unless you forget how to play properly, and want to come and be taught by us!'

'No, I don't, thank you,' said Allan. 'Goodbye.'

Allan went to the thick hedge that grew behind the little town of hillock houses, and squeezed his way through it. And on the other side was the field he knew so well – and his basket of games lying on the path!

Allan picked up the basket and set off to Michael's house. He was soon there, and Michael opened the door for him. 'What a long time you have been!' he said. 'Whatever have you been doing? Did you get lost?'

'No, not exactly lost,' said Allan, and he wouldn't say any more, for he was too ashamed to tell Michael all that had happened to him.

'Come along to the playroom and we will play our games there,' said Michael. 'We'll play draughts first.' So up they went, and set out the board on the playroom table. They put out the counters and began the game.

Michael was cleverer than Allan at the game, and soon took all his men – but do you suppose Allan cheated or lost his temper? No, not a bit of it! He said,

'You've won, Michael. Now let's play snap.'

So they got out the snap cards, and soon they were snapping away, taking each other's pile of cards. Allan thought of the way the goblins played snap with the puppy dog, and he couldn't help thinking that his and Michael's way was very much nicer!

'Snap!' said Michael suddenly, while Allan was thinking about the goblins and forgetting to look at the cards.

Oh! Michael had snapped all his pile of cards – and had won!

'It isn't fair,' said Allan, 'because I was just thinking about . . .'

And just as he spoke he thought he heard a little sound of a goblin chuckling away to himself. He looked round quickly. No, there wasn't a goblin to be seen.

'It's all right,' said Allan. 'It's quite fair. I should have been looking at the game.'

Then they began to play beat-your-neighbour-out-of-doors, and would you believe it, Michael seemed to have all the kings, queens and aces in the pack – so it wasn't very long before he had beaten Allan again. But this time the little boy was not going to say a word about the win not being fair – nor was he going to lose his temper!

'It's your game again!' he said to Michael. 'Jolly good!'

And he thought he heard a whisper somewhere, 'Jolly good, Allan! Well done!' But though he looked all round again, there was nobody there at all.

Allan plays games as they should be played now – no cheating, no grumbling, no losing of tempers. And one day he is going to squeeze through that thick hedge and tell those goblins something. He wants to say, 'Thank you for teaching me all you did! I'll never forget it.' Won't they be surprised?

Sneezing Powder

Sneezing Powder

ONCE UPON a time there lived a brownie called Smarty. He kept a little shop in Hallo Town, in which he sold jars of honey, fine yellow lemons and big yellow pills that helped to cure colds.

In the wintertime Smarty did a fine trade, for anyone who had a cold came to buy his honey, his juicy lemons and his cold pills. Then they would go home, squeeze the lemons into a glass, put in hot water and sugar and a spoonful or two of Smarty's golden honey, take a cold pill and go to bed – and lo and behold, the next morning they were cured!

But in the summertime nobody seemed to have a

cold at all. It was most annoying for Smarty. Instead of thinking of selling something else, such as ice creams or cool lemon drinks, Smarty still went on hoping that people would have colds and buy his cold cure. So he wasn't quite as smart as his name, was he?

He was quite smart enough to think out a naughty trick though!

If only I could make people think they had a cold, they would come and buy my honey and lemons and pills, thought Smarty. *If only they would sneeze or cough just as they passed my shop, it would be so easy for me to say, 'Dear me! You are getting a cold! Buy my cold cure before you are very bad!' But nobody ever sneezes outside my shop.*

Smarty sat and thought for a bit, and then he grinned all over his sly little face. He slapped his knee in delight. He had thought of a wonderful idea!

'I'll go and buy some sneezing powder from old Dame Flap!' he said to himself. 'And I'll put some into my pepperpot and shake it out of my bedroom window whenever anyone passes! Then they will sneeze hard and perhaps come and buy my goods.'

So off he went to buy the sneezing powder. He paid Dame Flap a silver coin for a boxful and she wrapped it up for him. It was a strange powder, rather like fine green flour, and it had a strange smell.

Smarty ran home with it. He emptied some into his pepperpot and slipped upstairs to his bedroom window, which was just over his shop. He leant out in excitement. Was anybody coming?

Yes, here was Old Man Shuffle! Smarty waited till he was underneath the window and then he shook out some of the powder. It went on Old Man Shuffle's nose, and he stopped. He took out his big blue handkerchief and held it to his nose.

'*Whooosh!*' he sneezed. '*A-whoosh!*'

'Hi, Old Man Shuffle, you've got a dreadful cold!' called Smarty. 'Come into my shop and get some honey and lemons and pills!'

So in shuffled the old fellow, thinking it was very lucky that he should be outside Smarty's shop just when his cold had begun. He bought a jar of honey, two lemons and a box of yellow pills. Smarty grinned. He ran up to his bedroom again.

'Ah! Here are Mr Twiddle and his wife!' chuckled Smarty. He shook his pepperpot over them. They stopped and fumbled for their hankies.

'*Er-tish-oo!*' said Mr Twiddle loudly.

'*Ish-ish-ish!*' sneezed Mrs Twiddle politely into her handkerchief.

'*ER-TISH-OOO!*' went Mr Twiddle.

'Not so much noise, Twiddle,' said Mrs Twiddle. '*Ish-ish-ish-ish!* Dear me! We are beginning colds, I think. Look, let's buy some honey and lemons, and maybe we'll stop our colds from getting worse.'

So into Smarty's shop they went and bought what they wanted, much to Smarty's delight. As soon as they had gone, he popped upstairs again with his pepperpot full of sneezing powder.

He made Twinkle the pixie sneeze and buy honey and pills. He made Mr Meddle sneeze so strongly that his hat flew on to the roof and he had to get a ladder to fetch it. He made Dame Winks sneeze twelve times, and at the end her bonnet was right over her nose and she couldn't see where she was going at all.

Oh, Smarty had plenty of fun that day, and he made plenty of money too! But when everyone found that they had no cold at all when they got home, and didn't need the honey and lemons, they were rather puzzled. They talked about it to one another, and they found that all of them had begun their sneezing fits outside Smarty's shop.

'Very nice for Smarty!' said Mr Meddle. 'Let us go along and see what we can see.'

So they all went back towards Smarty's shop, and peeped round the corner. And they saw Smarty leaning out of his bedroom window, pepperpot in hand!

'Aha!' Old Man Shuffle said angrily. 'So that's his trick, is it! Come along, everybody!'

They all went into Smarty's shop. Smarty hurried down to serve them. Mrs Twiddle was waiting for him. She snatched the pepperpot out of his pocket and shook it all over Smarty.

'Colds are catching today!' she said. 'Sneeze, Smarty, sneeze! Dear, dear! You must have caught our colds.'

'*Whoosh!*' said Smarty. '*Atish-o! Ish-ish-ish! Osha-whoosh! Tish-oo!*'

Mrs Twiddle emptied all the sneezing powder over him. My goodness, Smarty simply could not stop sneezing! It was dreadful!

'By the time you've finished I guess you'll want to buy a pot of your own honey, a dozen lemons and a box of pills!' said Mr Twiddle, laughing. 'Goodbye, Smarty. It serves you right!'

They all went out, giggling and chuckling, and they could hear Smarty's sneezes all the way down the road.

Poor Smarty! He sneezed all that day and all that night, and by that time his nose and throat and eyes were so sore that he had to take two jars of honey, six lemons and two of his own pills to cure himself!

Now he has shut up his shop and gone out selling ice creams. And a very much better idea too, in the summer – don't you think so?

Billy's Little Boats

Billy's Little Boats

ONCE UPON a time, not so very long ago, a crowd of little brownies had to leave their home hurriedly. They lived in Bluebell Wood, and one day it was sold to a builder. Alas for the brownies and the rabbits, the birds and the little mice – they all had to leave when the trees were chopped down, and the wood made ready for houses to be built all over it!

The birds flew to another wood. The rabbits fled to the hillside a mile away. The little mice held a meeting, and decided to hide somewhere till the houses were built, and then become house mice and live on food in the kitchens of the houses.

The brownies too held a meeting. They were very tiny folk, these brownies, so small that you could easily hold six in your hand together. They were small enough to use a violet leaf for an umbrella, so you can guess how tiny they were.

'We will go to our cousins, who live in Wishing Wood,' said the chief brownie, Chippy. 'I know the way quite well. You go through the wood, down the lane, across the river and up the hill. On the other side is Wishing Wood. It is a big place and there will be plenty of room for us to live there with our cousins.'

So one night they set off. They ran through their own spoilt wood. They went down the lane, which seemed simply enormous to them. Then they came to the river.

But here they had to stop in dismay. They hadn't thought at all how they were to cross it! Now what were they to do?

'We haven't wings, so we can't fly,' said Chippy.

'And there are no boats about,' said Tiggy.

'Not even a leaf or two we could use as a raft,' said Snippy.

'What shall we do?' said everyone together. 'We *must* get across tonight!'

A rabbit popped his head out of a nearby hole. 'What's the matter?' he said.

'Oh, can you help us?' asked the brownies, and they told the rabbit their trouble.

'No, I can't help you,' said the rabbit, shaking his whiskery head. 'But I know a very, very kind little boy called Billy, who lives in that house over there. He is very clever and *he* might help you. He once got me out of a trap. Go and knock at his window. He'll wake and do his best for you.'

It was moonlight and the brownies could see the window that the rabbit pointed to. It had bars across, for it was a nursery window. They thanked the rabbit and ran to the garden hedge, crept through it and ran to the house. They climbed up the thick ivy, and stood on Billy's windowsill. By the moonlight that shone into the room they could quite well see Billy, fast asleep in his small bed.

Chippy tapped at the window. Billy stirred. Chippy tapped again. Billy sat up, wide awake. When he saw the brownies at the window he was too astonished to speak. Then he jumped out of bed and ran to let them in.

'Oh!' he said. 'You dear tiny creatures! I've always longed to see the little folk – and now I really have. I do hope I'm awake and not dreaming!'

'Oh, you're awake all right,' said Chippy. 'Listen, Billy! A rabbit told us you were clever and kind. Do you think you could help us?'

'I can try,' said Billy at once. 'What do you want me to do?'

'Well,' said Chippy, 'we have to leave our home and we want to get to Wishing Wood, which is across the river and over the hill. We haven't wings to fly over the river, and we haven't boats. Could you tell us how to get across, please, Billy?'

Billy thought hard for a moment. 'Let me see,' he said. 'It's no use lending you my ship – it's far too big. And I've lost the oars of my little boat. And paper boats would soak with water and sink halfway across. Oh! I know! I've thought of just the right thing for you!'

'What? What?' cried the brownies excitedly.

'I'll make you walnut-shell boats!' said Billy. 'They'll be just the right size for you. One of you will go nicely into each. They float beautifully – and I can make you tiny sails so that the wind will blow you across!'

Billy ran downstairs. He had counted the brownies and there were eleven of them. He took six walnuts from the dish of nuts on the dining-room sideboard.

He ran upstairs again. He carefully slit each walnut into its two half-shells and took out the nut. He and the brownies chewed the nuts between them as Billy worked.

'Now, there you are!' said Billy when he had the

six shells empty, standing neatly in their halves. 'Twelve little boats! Good! Now I'll make the masts and the sails.'

He got out a box in which he kept all sorts of odds and ends. In it were a lot of dead matches. Billy was not allowed to touch proper matches, only ones that had already been struck, but he had quite a lot of these.

He took out a dead match and made holes in a small piece of white paper so that he could slip the bit of paper on the match for a sail! The match was the mast, you see. When he had got the sail nicely fixed he looked for his tube of Seccotine.

'What's that?' asked the brownies in surprise, as they saw Billy squeezing a tiny, sticky sort of worm out of the tube on to the end of the match.

'It's Seccotine – sticky stuff that sticks things together,' said Billy. 'This drop of Seccotine will stick the end of the match to the bottom of the walnut shell, you see, brownies – and then you will have a nice straight mast, with a dear little sail to catch the wind!'

The brownies were simply amazed to see Billy making them the dear little walnut-shell boats. Billy was so quick and so clever!

He stuck the match into the bottom of a shell. He arranged the bit of paper for a sail. The boat was ready!

'One boat done,' he said. 'Now for the next!'

As soon as the brownies saw how the boats were made, they began to help. Tiggy got in a bit of a mess with the Seccotine, which stuck to his hands, and then everything seemed to stick to *him*! Poor Tiggy!

It was not long before there were twelve boats finished. 'You only need eleven,' said Billy, 'but it would be quite a good idea to let the twelfth boat carry your bits of luggage. I can tie it on to one of the other boats.'

Soon Billy and the brownies were creeping quietly down the garden to the river. Billy carried all the boats on a tiny tray, for fear of spoiling them.

When he came to the river he set the tray down on the ground.

He launched one tiny boat, and it bobbed up and down beautifully on the ripples. The wind pulled at the tiny sail. Billy carefully put a brownie in the boat, and away it went, bobbing merrily over the river. Then another boat followed it, and another, and another – till the whole fleet was sailing away, looking perfectly lovely on the moonlit water.

The last but one had the twelfth luggage boat tied to the back of it. The two little boats bobbed safely away, the brownie in the first one waving goodbye. Billy stood and watched his fleet of walnut-shell boats sailing across to the other side, the wind blowing hard on the little paper sails. Not one boat sank.

'I do feel proud and pleased,' said Billy to himself. 'I've really done something tonight. I'll go to Wishing Wood some day and see if I can find those brownies again!'

He hasn't been yet, but I expect he will go soon. Would you like to make a fleet of walnut-shell boats like Billy? You can, easily. Sail them in the bath and they will look fine!

The Little Green Imp

The Little Green Imp

THE PRINCE of Ho-Ho had a very bad-tempered cook. None of the other servants liked her, but she was big and strong, and nobody dared to complain about her.

They had a very bad time until Twinkle, the kitchen boy, came to work there. Mrs Pudding, the cook, made him get up at five o'clock in the morning, and would not let him go to bed until midnight, and the poor boy was working hard all the time.

But Twinkle had a grandmother who was half a witch, and when he got out one afternoon to go on an errand he ran to his grandmother's cottage in the wood.

'Granny!' he said. 'Tell me what to do! There's a cook at the castle, and she gives me a dreadful time, and everyone else too! How can I stop her?'

His granny thought for a moment, and then she nodded her head. 'Wait a minute!' she said. 'I've just the thing for you!'

She took a big green dish and filled it full of water. She scattered a green powder into it and it changed the water to a brilliant emerald. She peeled a potato into it, stirred it round with a peacock's feather and muttered words so magical that Twinkle felt a bit frightened.

'Watch!' said his granny. He looked into a bowl, and suddenly out of the green water there jumped a green imp with a potato body and a grinning face! He smacked his hands together and looked up at Twinkle's grandmother.

'You'll do!' said the old lady, and she laughed.

'Here, Twinkle, put him into your pocket. As soon as you get into the kitchen, put him on a shelf and leave him. He will do the rest!'

Twinkle thanked his grandmother and put the green imp into his pocket. The imp laughed out loud and pinched him once or twice, but Twinkle didn't mind. He guessed that imp would play a few tricks on Mrs Pudding, the bad-tempered cook!

As soon as he got into the kitchen, he put the imp on the shelf behind a saucepan. Mrs Pudding turned round and scolded Twinkle. 'Why have you been so long, you good-for-nothing boy?'

'Now, Cookie, you be good!' said the voice of the green imp suddenly from the shelf. 'Naughty, naughty, naughty!'

Mrs Pudding turned round in a rage, too astonished to speak. The green imp peeped at her from behind a saucepan and made a face.

'And what are *you* doing in my kitchen, I'd like to know!' said Mrs Pudding, her eyes gleaming with rage. 'Come here!'

But that little imp stayed where he was, rapping out a tune on one of the saucepans and grinning with all his might. 'Oh, Cookie, what a naughty temper!' he shouted.

The other servants were all staring in delight and astonishment. How could that green imp dare to speak to Mrs Pudding like that? The cook went over to the shelf and put out her hand to get the imp, but he picked up a fork lying nearby and rapped her fingers hard. Then he pushed six saucepans on to the floor, one after another . . . Bang! Crash! Smash! Bang! Crash! Smash! What a dreadful noise they made! Mrs Pudding was very angry.

She picked up a newspaper and folded it so that she might hit the little imp with it. She brought it down on the shelf . . . bang! Two more saucepans and a kettle jumped off to the ground . . . Bang! Crash! Clang! The imp was nowhere to be seen.

'That's finished *him*!' said Mrs Pudding, pleased.

But, dear me, it hadn't. No, he had just jumped neatly off the shelf on to the kitchen table behind the cook. And on the table he saw a jug of milk. The imp grinned. He picked it up by the handle, jumped up on to the mantelpiece and tilted the jug over Mrs Pudding's head.

Trickle, trickle, trickle! The milk fell on her head and ran down her neck! She got such a shock! How that imp laughed! He nearly fell off the mantelpiece with laughing. As for Twinkle and the other servants, they roared too. But Mrs Pudding got angrier and angrier.

She picked up a large cabbage and flung it at the imp. He dodged it neatly and it hit the kitchen clock. Crash! Down came the clock and a big tea caddy, and the cabbage too! The cook stared in horror!

'Oh, naughty, naughty, naughty!' said the imp, dancing about on the table, on to which he had jumped again.

Mrs Pudding turned round to him, and the wicked

little thing threw an egg at her. It broke and went down her neck to join the milk. Oh, dear – poor Mrs Pudding! What a sight she looked! The imp began to laugh so much that he was afraid he might be caught, so he jumped up on to another shelf and hid in a bucket there. Mrs Pudding looked all round for him, and when she could not find him she went to wash the egg off herself.

'How dare you all stand grinning there?' she cried to the other servants. 'Get on with your work at once, and if you see that green imp anywhere about just catch him and bring him to me!'

But nobody meant to catch him. It was fun to see someone who was not afraid of Mrs Pudding! She washed herself and then scolded Twinkle for upsetting some salt.

'Oh, naughty Cookie, oh, naughty Cookie!' squealed the voice of the green imp, and he popped his head out of the bucket. Mrs Pudding saw him.

'Oh, so you've turned up again, have you?' she

said. 'Well, I'll get you this time!'

And with that she took the bucket down from the shelf, but the imp hopped out and ran into the larder crying, 'Can't catch *me*, can't catch *me*!'

Mrs Pudding rushed after him, but he was waiting for her. He threw a string of sausages round her neck and dropped a pat of butter neatly on her head from the top shelf. Really, you never knew what that wicked imp was going to do next!

All the evening things went on like that, and there was no catching that imp, and no stopping him either. Twice he emptied water over Mrs Pudding, and once he pelted her with apples he had found in a basket. Mrs Pudding rushed round and round the kitchen after him, but she couldn't seem to get hold of him at all. He was as slippery as an eel. He undid her shoelaces when she wasn't looking. He undid her apron strings and made her apron slip off a dozen times. He emptied pepper near her, and she sneezed thirty times without stopping.

'Oh, won't someone get rid of this horrid little imp for me!' wept Mrs Pudding at last. 'What has he come for?'

'I think he has come to tease you and torment you because you have treated *us* so badly,' said Twinkle boldly.

'That's right, that's right, that's right!' squealed the imp from somewhere under the table, where he was busy untying Mrs Pudding's shoes again.

'If only you'd catch him and get rid of him for me, I'd mend my ways and be better,' sobbed Mrs Pudding, who was quite tired out.

'Very well then, I'll try,' said Twinkle, grinning to himself. He knew just what to do, for his granny had told him. He took a pat of butter, a dab of vinegar and a brown clove. He stuck the clove into the butter and smeared it with vinegar. Then he held it out to the imp.

The little green imp smelt the clove in the butter and came eagerly for it. Twinkle snatched him up and put him into his pocket.

'I'll go and give him to my old granny,' he said to Mrs Pudding. 'She will know what to do with him, for she is half a witch.'

He ran off, chuckling to himself, and soon came to his grandmother's. When she heard his story, how she laughed! 'That will cure her bad temper!' she said. 'Tell Mrs Pudding that I will take the imp, but I shall not be able to keep him if she loses her temper again, for he will surely come back!'

So Twinkle left the green imp with his granny, who set him to work polishing her kettles and saucepans until they shone. He was afraid to do anything cheeky to the old dame. She had made him from a potato, and she could turn him back into one again!

As for Mrs Pudding, she didn't dare to lose her temper again, for she was so afraid the imp would turn up in her kitchen once more. So now all is peace and quiet there, and Twinkle the kitchen boy is as happy as can be.

But he can't help wishing Mrs Pudding would lose her temper once or twice – it *would* be such fun to see that imp dodging about the kitchen shouting, 'Naughty Cookie! Naughty, naughty!' at the top of his cheeky little voice. I'd rather like to see him myself, wouldn't you?

The Wishing Hat

The Wishing Hat

SPILLIKINS THE pixie went into Dame Twinkle's teashop for tea. He took off his pointed cap and hung it up on a hook behind his chair. Then he ordered tea.

He looked round the shop. There were quite a lot of people there. He saw See-Saw the wizard, eating sardines on gingerbread, a meal he liked very much. He saw Whistler the gnome drinking pink lemonade. And in the corner were Flip and Flap the goblins, eating egg pie as fast as they could.

Spillikins was in rather a hurry so he asked for a glass of cold milk and a bun. He knew they wouldn't take very long to prepare. He munched his bun, and when it was finished he drank his milk down to the last drop. Then he paid his bill, took his cap off the hook, popped it on his head and off he went.

It was a bright and beautiful sunny day and Spillikins whistled cheerily as he thought of the day ahead. He was going to see his friend Tippy, who lived in a lovely little cottage all by himself. Spillikins was going to help him to weed his garden. Tippy lived a long way away, and Spillikins soon got hot walking along in the sunshine that streamed over the fields.

'I wish somebody would come to wheel me in a barrow all the way there,' he said to himself. 'I'm getting jolly hot.'

Just as he said that he heard something trundling behind him. He turned round – and what a funny thing! There was a big green wheelbarrow being pushed by an imp. He knocked Spillikins into the barrow and began to wheel him along.

'Ooh!' said Spillikins in surprise. 'He must have

heard what I said, and decided to give me a ride. Well, this is better than walking.'

The imp pushed him along, over the field and down the lanes. Spillikins liked it – but the barrow was very hard to sit in, especially when it bumped over stones.

'I do wish I had a nice cushion or something to sit on,' he said. 'I'm getting quite bruised.'

No sooner had he said the words than to his enormous surprise a huge yellow cushion appeared under him in the barrow! It was so soft and comfortable. Spillikins stared at it in amazement.

'Well, where did you come from?' he asked. 'Hi, imp! Did you put this cushion here?'

But the imp said nothing. He just went on wheeling the barrow. Spillikins looked puzzled. There was something funny about the imp and the sudden way he had appeared.

'I am hot!' sighed the pixie, as the sun shone down hotter than ever. 'I wish it would rain lemonade. How nice it would–'

He stopped suddenly. A great yellow cloud had blown over the sun, and large yellow drops of rain had started to fall all around.

'Buttons and buttercups!' cried Spillikins in astonishment. 'I do believe it is raining lemonade. Ooh, what a funny thing!'

He opened his mouth and let the drops fall on to his tongue. They were delicious. Real, sweet lemonade, the nicest he had ever tasted. But after a while Spillikins began to feel wet, for the lemonade shower was a heavy one.

'I wish it would stop,' he said. 'I'm getting wet through.'

In an instant the lemonade rain stopped and the sky became blue again. Spillikins looked very thoughtful. It was turning into a very strange day indeed.

'It seems to me as if all my wishes are coming true,' he said. 'I wonder why. Well, I'll wish a few more and see if they come true too.'

He thought for a moment. Then he wished.

'I wish I had a carriage made of gold, drawn by three giraffes,' he said.

Immediately a shining carriage stood before him, and in front were three tall giraffes! Spillikins was delighted. He jumped out of the wheelbarrow and ran to the carriage.

'I wish for a lion to drive my carriage and two kangaroos for footmen,' he said.

Immediately the wish came true. A lion sat on the box, dressed in a wonderful coachman's uniform, and two kangaroos dressed as footmen stood up behind.

'Now I wish for a suit of gold and a cloak of silver,' said Spillikins. 'Ha! Here they are! Don't I look grand!'

He got into the carriage and told the lion to drive to his friend Tippy's house. He wished for all sorts of animals to follow him, all dressed in silver tunics and each carrying a present for his friend, and to his great delight they appeared, looking very grand indeed. There was an elephant, a camel with a present between his humps, a big furry panda and even an ostrich!

That will make Tippy stare, thought Spillikins in delight. *He's always boasting about this, that and the other – but he won't boast any more when he sees me! I've only got to wish and I can have anything I want!*

He was so excited that he could hardly wait to get to Tippy's. When at last the giraffe coach drew up outside his friend's cottage he saw Tippy in the garden. But as soon as Tippy saw the lion coachman, the giraffes and the kangaroo footmen, he dropped his spade and fled indoors, frightened out of his life!

'Hi, Tippy! Tippy! Don't be afraid!' cried Spillikins. 'It's only me! Guess what! All my wishes are coming true!'

He ran indoors after Tippy and told him everything that had happened, and at last his friend believed him. He kept staring and staring at Spillikins in his gold tunic and silver cloak, and he wondered how it was that the pixie had managed to make his wishes come true.

'I don't know *how* it is,' said Spillikins. 'I really don't. It must just be some wonderful magic that has grown in me.'

'Take off your hat and sit down,' said Tippy. 'You have had such a busy day. And besides, we don't need to do any weeding. We can just wish all the weeds away, and our work will be done. Ha ha!'

'Ha, ha!' said Spillikins, and he pulled off his pointed cap.

'I say!' he said, staring at it. 'This cap isn't mine! I must have taken the wrong one at the teashop. No wonder it felt so tight! It doesn't fit me at all well, and has given me quite a headache. I wish I had my own cap instead.'

Whoooooooosh! Almost before he had finished speaking, the cap he was holding flew away suddenly and another cap fell into Spillikins' hands. It was his own! But oh, dear me, at the very same moment away went his silver cloak and gold tunic, leaving him in his plain old clothes. Off galloped the giraffe coach, and after it went all the animals with the presents Spillikins had brought for Tippy!

'Oh my, what's happening?' cried Spillikins, all of a tremble. 'Hi! I wish you all to come back.'

But alas! They didn't come back. They had gone for good!

'Oh, dear, dear, dear!' sobbed Spillikins in the greatest disappointment. 'I know what's happened. I must have taken Wizard See-Saw's hat by mistake when I left the teashop. It was a wishing cap – and that's why all the wishes I wished came true. Now I've got my own cap back I've lost the wishing power!'

'Oh!' groaned Tippy, getting up, 'And to think we might have wished all those weeds away! Why didn't we when we had the chance? Come along out, Spilly, and do some work.'

Out they went, two very sad little pixies. That night they both dreamt of lions, kangaroos and giraffes – and I don't wonder at it, do you?

The Kickaway Shoes

The

SKIP AND JUMP were very busy brownies. They had been spring-cleaning their cottage from top to bottom – and my, what a lot of rubbish they had turned out!

'Look at that!' said Skip, pointing to an enormous pile of old kettles, old books and old boots and shoes he had put in their back garden. 'Whatever are we going to do with all this rubbish?'

'And look at my pile of rubbish too!' said Jump. Skip looked. It certainly was an even bigger pile than his. There was a broken-down iron bedstead, two chipped vases, an old enamel candlestick, four saucepans with holes in . . . oh, and heaps more things.

going to do with them?' asked Skip.

n them; they won't burn.'

e haven't a dustman in our village,' said

So we can't ask him to collect our rubbish.'

nd we are *not* going to throw these old things

o the ditches, as lots of untidy people do,' said Skip. 'That would spoil the countryside. So what *are* we to do?'

'I say, what about borrowing those Kickaway Shoes belonging to old Grumpy Gnome!' cried Jump at once. 'They would soon take all our rubbish away!'

'Ooh, yes,' said Skip. 'But I'm afraid of the Grumpy Gnome. He's so bad-tempered, and I don't trust him.'

'Well, if we pay him for the loan of his magic shoes, he can't be angry with us,' said Jump. 'Just think, Skip! Whatever we kick with the Kickaway Shoes immediately disappears! It's wonderful! If I kicked that old saucepan there with a Kickaway Shoe, it would fly away and we'd never see it again! Ooh, it wouldn't take us long to get rid of all our rubbish then, would it?'

'And what fun it would be to do some magic kicking!' cried Skip, jumping about in excitement. 'What fun! Let's go and ask Grumpy Gnome now.'

'We'll take a piece of gold with us,' said Jump, running to his purse, which was on the mantelpiece. 'He is sure to charge us a lot. He is a greedy, selfish, horrid fellow, and nobody likes him. We won't stay long, in case he puts a nasty spell on us.'

Off went the two brownies in great excitement. Jump had the piece of gold safely in his pocket. They soon came to Grumpy's cottage. It was built into the hillside, and there was a red door with a big black knocker. Jump knocked loudly. Rat-tat-tat!

The Grumpy Gnome opened the door and glared at them. He was a nasty-looking person. He had yellow whiskers and a very long nose. His eyes were small and he wore on his head a round red cap with little silver bells all along the rim. They rang when he walked. It was a magic cap, and he never took it off, not even to brush his hair. So nobody knew whether he had any hair or not.

'What do you want?' he said in his loud, deep voice.

'Please would you lend us your Kickaway Shoes?' asked Jump politely. 'We will pay you for the loan of them.'

'I shall want a piece of gold,' said the Grumpy Gnome, nodding his head till all the silver bells on his cap rang loudly.

'We have brought you a piece,' said Jump, and he showed the gold to Grumpy. The gnome's little eyes shone at the sight of the gold, and he suddenly grabbed it and put it into his own pocket.

'Here are the shoes,' he said, taking down a curious pair of shoes from a shelf behind the door. They were bright yellow, and had turned-up ends of red-painted iron to kick with. The two brownies took them eagerly. They thanked the gnome and turned to go.

'Bring them back tonight without fail,' commanded

Grumpy. He shook his head fiercely at them, making all the silver bells tinkle again, and then slammed the door.

'What an unpleasant creature he is, to be sure,' said Skip, looking quite pale. 'I was really afraid he was going to turn us into black beetles or something! You know, he is supposed to do that to people he doesn't like. And once he turned a cheeky pixie into a currant bun and ate him! Oooh my, he's a horrid person!'

The brownies hurried home with the magic shoes. When they got there they each put a shoe on their right foot and danced about in glee.

'We've got the Kickaway Shoes, we've got the Kickaway Shoes!' they cried. They made such a noise that Whiskers, their big black cat, came out to see what they were doing.

'Hallo, Whiskers, darling!' cried the brownies, who were both very fond of their cat. 'Look at our magic shoes.'

Whiskers sniffed at them and then hurriedly

backed away. She had smelt the magic in them and was afraid. She went off to a corner of the garden.

'Now let's start kicking away all our rubbish!' cried Skip. 'Come on! Watch me kick away this old saucepan!'

He stood behind the saucepan, lifted his right foot and gave the saucepan an enormous kick with the iron end of the Kickaway Shoe! Bang!

The saucepan shot into the air and flew away! My, how it flew! The brownies watched it going through the air until it was just a black speck. Then they couldn't see it any longer.

'I wonder where it's gone to,' said Jump.

'It's gone to the Land of Rubbish,' said Skip. 'Now it's your turn, Jump. Kick that vase away!'

Jump kicked with all his might. The vase broke into a hundred pieces, and each piece flew through the air at top speed. They soon disappeared. The brownies giggled. This was great fun!

'We'll both kick away this nasty old bedstead,'

said Skip. 'It's so big it wants two people to kick it, I'm sure!'

They both kicked with all their might. At once the bedstead rose into the air, and to the great delight of the brownies, and to the enormous surprise of the pixies down in the village, the old iron bedstead flew off through the air, looking smaller and smaller the further it flew. It was most exciting.

The brownies laughed till the tears came into their eyes. They were having a glorious time. They kicked away the candlesticks, the old boots and the tin kettles. They kicked away a pile of books and a broken spade. They kicked dozens of things and shouted in glee when they saw them all flying off in the air, never to come back.

At last there was nothing but an old basket left. Skip gave it a hard kick, and it rose into the air – but oh, goodness, what a dreadful thing! Whiskers, the cat, had curled herself up in that basket and Skip didn't know she was there! When the basket rose up in the air Whiskers shot out and she and the basket flew along together at top speed!

Whiskers mewed loudly, but it was no use. She had to go to the Land of Rubbish, and soon the horrified brownies could see nothing of her but a tiny black speck far away in the sky.

'Oh! Oh!' cried Skip, the tears running down his cheeks in two streams. 'I didn't know Whiskers was in the basket! She'll never come back! Oh, my dear, darling old cat! Oh, Jump, she's gone!'

Jump sobbed too. Both brownies loved their cat with all their hearts, and it was dreadful to think poor old Whiskers had been kicked off to the Land of Rubbish. How upset she would be! How lonely and frightened!

'Who will g-g-g-give her her m-m-m-m-milk?' wept Skip.

'Who will t-t-t-t-tuck her up in a warm rug at night?' sobbed Jump.

It was dreadful. The brownies couldn't think

what to do! They put their arms round one another and cried so much that they made a puddle round their feet.

At last Skip had an idea.

'Let's go to Grumpy Gnome and ask him to tell us how to get Whiskers back!' he said. 'There is sure to be a spell to get her back.'

'Yes, yes!' cried Jump, wiping his eyes with his big yellow handkerchief. So off they set once more to Grumpy's cottage.

The gnome frowned at them when he opened the door.

'I said bring back the shoes tonight, not this afternoon,' he said crossly. 'I was just having a nap and you've wakened me.'

'Oh, please, Grumpy, we've come about something terribly important,' said Skip. 'We kicked Whiskers, our lovely black cat, away by mistake, and we want you to tell us how to get her back!'

Grumpy's little eyes gleamed. *Ha!* he thought.

I can make some money out of this.

'Well,' he said aloud. 'That's certainly very serious. You will have to pay me a very large sum of money to get her back. It's very hard to get a black cat back from the Land of Rubbish.'

'Oh, dear,' said Jump and Skip. 'How much money do you want?'

'I want fifty pieces of gold!' said Grumpy.

'Ooooooo!' squealed Skip and Jump in horror. 'We only have three pieces! Get us our cat back for three pieces, Grumpy.'

'Certainly not,' said the gnome, pretending that he was shutting the door. 'Fifty pieces, or no cat!'

'Wait, wait!' said Jump. 'We've only three pieces, I tell you. What else will you take besides our three pieces of gold?'

'Well, I'll take your grandfather clock,' said Grumpy.

'Oh!' groaned the brownies sorrowfully. 'We do so love our old clock. But you shall have it.'

'And your rocking chair,' said Grumpy. 'And the pair of lovely brass candlesticks you have on your mantelpiece.'

The brownies groaned again. They were proud of their rocking chair and candlesticks. But still, they loved Whiskers more than all these things, so they sadly promised to go back home and fetch the gold, the clock, the chair and the candlesticks at once.

They ran off, crying. What a dreadful thing to have to give up all their nicest things to the horrid, greedy gnome! If he had been at all kind-hearted he would have been sorry about Whiskers, and would have got her back for nothing. But oh, Grumpy Gnome had a heart as hard as stone!

Skip and Jump fetched out their big clock, their old rocking chair, and the two candlesticks. Skip had the gold in his pocket. He carried the rocking chair too. Jump managed to take the grandfather clock and the candlesticks. They went slowly along, panting and puffing under their heavy loads.

Just as they got near Grumpy's cottage they met Bron, the head brownie of the village. He was most astonished to see Skip and Jump carrying such heavy things.

'Are you moving?' he asked.

'No,' said Skip. 'We are taking these to Grumpy.' Then he told Bron all that had happened, and how Grumpy had made them promise to give him their nicest things in return for getting back Whiskers from the Land of Rubbish.

'So that's why we are taking him our three gold pieces, our beautiful grandfather clock, our rocking chair and our lovely candlesticks,' said Skip sadly. 'But you see, we must get Whiskers back. She'll be so lonely and so frightened.'

Bron frowned and looked as black as thunder when he heard about the greed and selfishness of the unkind gnome.

'Where are the Kickaway Shoes?' he asked.

'I've still got one on, and so has Skip,' said Jump,

and he lifted up his right foot to show Bron.

'Give them to me,' said Bron.

In great surprise Skip and Jump took off the Kickaway Shoes and watched Bron put them on, one on each foot. Then they looked on in even greater surprise when he marched straight up to Grumpy's front door and banged hard on the knocker.

RAT-A-TAT-TAT!

The door flew open and out came Grumpy, looking very angry indeed.

'How dare you knock so loudly!' he began in a rage – then he stopped when he saw it was Bron knocking and not Skip and Jump.

'I've just come to tell you something, Grumpy Gnome,' said Bron in a very fierce voice. 'I've come to tell you that you are the nastiest, greediest, unkindest gnome in the whole of the kingdom, and you don't deserve to live in this nice little village.'

'Oh, don't I?' said Grumpy, his little eyes glittering wickedly. 'Well, where do I deserve to live then? Tell me that!' And he turned to go indoors again.

'The best place for you is the Land of Rubbish!' shouted Bron, and before Grumpy could get inside his door, he kicked him hard with the iron points of the Kickaway Shoes – first with one shoe and then with the other.

Oh, my goodness me! Grumpy gave a loud yell and rose up into the air, and then, still yelling, he flew on and on to the Land of Rubbish. The brownies watched him – and then suddenly Skip gave a cry.

'Oh, Bron! You've kicked him away before he told us how to get back dear old Whiskers. Oh, dear, oh, dear!'

'Don't worry!' said Bron cheerfully. 'A cat can always find its way home again, no matter where it's taken to. Whiskers will come back all right – and that wicked gnome knew it perfectly well. He was just robbing you of all these things for nothing. Take them back home again, put down a saucer of milk and wait for Whiskers to come back.'

'Oh, thank you, Bron,' said the grateful little brownies. 'But what are you going to do with the Kickaway Shoes?'

'I shall keep them in my house, and then if anyone wants to borrow them he can do so for nothing,' said Bron. He put on his own shoes, and then, taking the Kickaway Shoes under his arm, he went off home, whistling loudly. He stopped every now and then to laugh when he thought of Grumpy Gnome sailing through the air to the Land of Rubbish!

Skip and Jump staggered home again with all their belongings. They put them back in their places, and then they went to the larder for some milk. They poured out a saucerful and put it down on the floor, ready for Whiskers when she came back.

Then they put the kettle on for tea, and toasted some muffins, for they really felt very hungry.

And would you believe it, just as they were sitting down to eat their tea, there came a mewing at the door! Skip leapt up and opened it – and there outside was dear old Whiskers, very tired and very hungry, for she had walked a very long way indeed.

'Darling old Whiskers!' cried the brownies in delight, hugging her and stroking her soft fur. 'Oh, we are glad to see you! Here's some milk for you! And shall we open a tin of sardines for you, just for a treat?'

They were all so happy that evening. Whiskers sat on Skip's knee first, and then on Jump's, so that they might share her properly between them. She was just as glad to be back again as they were to have her.

As for Grumpy Gnome, he's still in the Land of Rubbish. And a very good place for him too!

The Witch's Cat

The Witch's Cat

OLD DAME KIRRI was a witch. You could tell she was because she had bright green eyes. She was a good witch though, and spent most of her time making good spells to help people who were ill or unhappy.

She lived in Toppling Cottage, which was just like its name and looked exactly as if it was going to topple over. But it was kept up by strong magic and not a brick had fallen, although the cottage was five hundred years old.

At the back of the cottage was the witch's garden. Round it ran a very, very high wall, taller than the tallest man.

'I like a high wall. It keeps people from peeping and prying,' said old Witch Kirri. 'In my garden I grow a lot of strange and powerful herbs. I don't want people to see them and steal them. I won't have people making spells from my magic herbs – they might make bad ones.'

The witch had a cat. It was black and big, and had green eyes very like the witch's. Its name was Cinder-Boy.

Cinder-Boy helped the witch with her spells. He was really a remarkably clever cat. He knew how to sit exactly in the middle of a chalk ring without moving, while Kirri the witch danced round and sang spells. He knew how to go out and collect dewdrops in the moonlight. He took a special little silver cup for that, and never spilt a drop. He never drank milk. He liked tea, made as strong as the witch made for herself. Sometimes he would sit and sip his tea and purr, and the witch would sip her tea and purr too. It was funny to see them.

Cinder-Boy loved to sleep in the walled-in garden. He knew all the flowers and herbs which grew there. No weeds were allowed to grow. Cinder-Boy scratched them all up.

But one day he came to a small plant growing at the foot of the wall. It had leaves like a rose bush. It had pale pink flowers, with a mass of yellow stamens in the middle. It smelt very sweet.

'What flower are you?' said Cinder-Boy. 'You smell rather like a rose.'

'Well, that's just what I am,' said the plant. 'I'm a wild rose.'

'How did you get here?' said Cinder-Boy, surprised.

'A bird dropped a seed,' said the wild rose. 'But I don't like being here, black cat.'

'My name is Cinder-Boy,' said the witch's cat. 'Why don't you like being here? It is a very nice place to be.'

'Well, I feel shut in,' said the wild rose. 'I'm not very large. If I was taller than the wall I could grow up into the air, and see over the top. I don't like being down here at the bottom, shut in.'

'Well, grow tall then,' said Cinder-Boy. 'I can give you a spell to make your stems nice and long, if you like. Then you can reach up to the top of the wall and look over. There's a nice view there, I can tell you.'

'Oh, would you do that?' said the wild rose in delight. 'Thank you!'

So Cinder-Boy went off to get a spell which would make the stems of the wild rose grow very long. He soon found one. It was in a small blue bottle, and he poured it into a watering can. The spell was blue too.

Then he watered the wild rose with the spell, and it began to work almost at once. In two or three days the stems of the wild rose plant had grown quite high into the air.

'Go on growing. You will soon be at the top of the wall!' said Cinder-Boy. So the wild rose went on, making its stems longer and longer, hoping to get to the very top of the wall.

But when Cinder-Boy next strolled out into the

garden to see how it was getting on, what a shock he had! Every single stem was bent over and lay sprawling over the grass!

'Why, what has happened?' said Cinder-Boy, waving his tail in surprise.

'My stalks grew tall, but they didn't grow strong,' said the wild rose sadly. 'Just as I reached the top of the wall, they all flopped over and fell down. They are not strong enough to bear their own weight.'

'Well, how do plants with weak stems manage to climb high then?' said Cinder-Boy, puzzled. 'Runner beans grow high and they have very weak stems. Sweet peas grow high, and they have weak stems too. I'll go and see how they do it.' So off he went, for the witch grew both in the garden. He soon came back.

'The beans twine their stalks round poles,' he said, 'and the sweet peas grow little green fingers, called tendrils, which catch hold of things, and they pull themselves up high like that. Can't you do that?'

The wild rose couldn't. It didn't know how to. Its

stems wouldn't twist themselves, however much it tried to make them do so. And it couldn't grow a tendril at all.

'Well, we must think of another way,' said the cat.

'Cinder-Boy, how do you get up to the top of the wall?' asked the wild rose. 'You are often up there in the sun. I see you. Well, how do you get to the top?'

'I run up the trees,' said Cinder-Boy. 'Do you see the young fruit trees near you? Well, I run up those to the top of the wall. I use my claws to help me. I dig them into the bark of the trees, and hold on with them.'

He showed the wild rose his big, curved claws. 'I can put them in or out as I like,' he said. 'They are very useful claws.'

The wild rose thought they were too. 'If I grew claws like that I could easily climb up the fruit trees, right through them to the top, and then I'd be waving at the top of the wall,' it said. 'Can't you get me some claws like yours, Cinder-Boy?'

The cat blinked his green eyes and thought hard. 'I know what I could do,' he said. 'I could ask Witch Kirri, my mistress, to make some magic claws that would grow on you. I'll ask her today. In return you must promise to grow her some lovely scarlet rosehips which she can trim her hats and bonnets with in the autumn.'

'Oh, I will, I will,' promised the wild rose. So Cinder-Boy went off to Witch Kirri and asked her for what he wanted.

She grumbled a little. 'It is difficult to make claws,' she said. 'Very difficult. You will have to help me, Cinder-Boy. You will have to sit in the middle of a blue ring of chalk, and put out all your claws at once, while I sing a magic song. Don't be scared at what happens.'

In the middle of the garden the witch drew a chalk ring and Cinder-Boy went to sit in the middle of it. He stuck out all his claws as she commanded and she danced round with her broomstick singing such a magic song that Cinder-Boy felt quite scared. Then a funny thing happened.

His claws fell out on to the ground with a clatter – and they turned red or green as they fell. He looked at his paws and saw new ones growing. Then those fell out too. How very, very strange!

Soon there was quite a pile of claws on the ground. Then the witch stopped singing and dancing, and rubbed out the ring of chalk.

'You can come out now, Cinder-Boy,' she said. 'The magic is finished.'

Cinder-Boy collected all the red and green claws. They were strong and curved and sharp. He took them to the bottom of the garden, and came to the wild rose.

'I've got claws for you!' he said. 'Witch Kirri did some strong magic. Look, here they are. I'll press each one into your stems, till you have claws all down them. Then I'll say a growing spell, and they will grow into you properly and belong to you.'

So Cinder-Boy did that, and the wild rose felt the cat claws growing firmly into the long stems.

'Now,' said Cinder-Boy in excitement, 'now you will be able to climb up through the fruit trees, wild rose. I will help you at first.'

So Cinder-Boy took the wild rose stems, all set with claws, and pushed them up into the little fruit tree that grew nearby. The claws took hold of the bark and held on firmly. Soon all the stems were climbing up high through the little fruit tree, the claws digging themselves into the trunk and the branches.

The wild rose grew higher. It pulled itself up by its new claws. It was soon at the top of the wall! It could see right over it to the big world beyond.

'Now I'm happy!' said the wild rose to Cinder-Boy. 'Come and sit up here on the wall beside me. Let us look at the big world together. Oh, Cinder-Boy, it is lovely up here. I am not shut in any longer. Thank you for my claws. I do hope I shall go on growing them now.'

It did. And it grew beautiful scarlet berries in the autumn, for Witch Kirri's winter bonnets. You should see how pretty they are when she trims them with the rosehips!

Ever since that day the wild roses have grown cat claws all down their stems, sometimes green and sometimes red or pink. They use them to climb with. Have you seen them? If you haven't, do go and look. It will surprise you to see cat claws growing out of a plant!

It was a good idea of Cinder-Boy's, wasn't it?

The Yellow Trumpets

The Yellow Trumpets

ONCE UPON a time there were two little elves called Flip and Pinkle who lived in Fairyland and made trumpets. They made all sorts of lovely trumpets – big ones, little ones, long ones, short ones, white ones, red ones and blue ones.

They sold them as fast as they made them, because the baby fairies loved blowing them, and were always coming to buy them.

'One penny, please,' said Flip, giving a brownie a red one.

All day long they sold them in their little shop, and when night came they shut the shop and sat down to make more.

Soon every fairy baby, little elf and tiny pixie had a trumpet, and you should have heard the noise in the streets and houses of Fairyland.

Tan-tan-tara! Tan-tan-tara!

It was the baby trumpeters blowing their trumpets.

The older fairies didn't mind at first. They liked the babies to amuse themselves and have fun. They put up with the noise and laughed.

But one day Pinkle discovered a way to make a trumpet which made such a loud noise that any passerby nearly jumped out of his skin when he heard it!

It was a large, wide, yellow trumpet, beautifully made. Pinkle was very pleased with it.

'Flip!' he called. 'Come here and see my new trumpet!'

Flip hurried to see it. Pinkle showed the trumpet to him, then hid himself beside the window.

When a gnome came hurrying by the window,

carrying his morning's shopping, Pinkle blew his yellow trumpet loudly.

Tan-tan-tan-TARA! it went, right in the gnome's ear. He had never in his life heard such a tremendous noise.

He jumped into the air in fright, dropped his basket of shopping and went scurrying down the street as fast as he could, feeling quite sure that some dreadful animal was roaring at him.

Pinkle and Flip laughed till they cried.

'Let's show the trumpet to the babies!' said Pinkle. 'They're sure to want one each, and we will charge them sixpence!'

'Oh yes,' said Flip in delight.

'Then we will be so rich that we'll never need to make any more trumpets, and we'll go away and have a lazy time for the rest of our lives!'

So the two naughty elves showed the baby fairies their new trumpet, and told them what fun they could have frightening everyone.

The little fairies thought it was a lovely idea, and sounded like great fun, and so did the baby pixies. They asked Pinkle and Flip to make them each one, and agreed that they would pay them sixpence.

So the two elves set to work, and by the next day they had made twelve, and sold them all for sixpence each.

Then what a noise there was in the streets of Fairyland!

Tan-tan-TARA! Tan-tan-TARA!

The new trumpets nearly deafened everyone, and made people jump in fright.

'This won't do at all,' said the king of the fairies. 'We must stop this. We don't mind the little trumpets, but these big trumpets are too noisy. Pinkle and Flip must not make any more.'

So a message was sent to tell the two elves they must not make any more of the big yellow trumpets.

They were terribly disappointed. What a shame not to make any more, just as they were getting so rich through selling them! Oh, dear, oh, dear!

Pinkle and Flip talked about the message very crossly, and then Flip suddenly whispered something in Pinkle's big left ear.

'Let's go on making them and selling them anyway. We'll tell the customers to come at night, and no one will know. Shall we, Pinkle?' Pinkle nodded.

'Yes! We won't take any notice of the silly message. We'll make lots and lots more, and sell them every night when it's dark.'

So when their little customers came to the shop the naughty elves whispered to them to come and buy their yellow trumpets at midnight, if they really badly wanted them.

And night after night, naughty little fairies and mischievous little pixies came creeping to Pinkle's back door, paid sixpence and took away a trumpet.

Pinkle and Flip became richer and richer, and Fairyland became noisier and noisier.

At last the older fairies became really angry. They

couldn't even sleep at night because of all the noise. But although they watched Pinkle and Flip's shop carefully every single day, they never once saw the elves sell one of those big yellow trumpets that made such a dreadful noise. They couldn't understand it. Where did the trumpets come from if Pinkle and Flip didn't make them?

'I know what we'll do,' said one of the fairies. 'We'll go to Flip and Pinkle's shop, and search it from top to bottom. Then we shall know if they have been making the trumpets. If they haven't, we must look somewhere else! We'll go as soon as the shop is open tomorrow!'

Now, that night when a little elf came to buy a trumpet, he told them what he had heard, and the two naughty elves were terribly frightened.

They knew that if they were found out, they might be sent right away from Fairyland, and they didn't want that to happen.

'What shall we do, what shall we do?' cried Pinkle. 'We've nowhere to hide the trumpets!'

Flip thought for a minute.

'I know,' he said, 'we'll hide them in the fields. Quick, bring as many as you can!'

The two elves hurried out to the fields, where a great many yellow flowers were growing.

'If we stick our trumpets into the middle of these yellow flowers, no one will guess where they are!' said Flip. 'Come on!'

And quickly he began pushing a big yellow trumpet into each yellow-petalled flower. They matched beautifully!

When all the trumpets were hidden the two elves went back to their shop. It was just time to open it, so they unbolted the door.

In came the king of the fairies, and told Pinkle and Flip they were going to search the house from top to bottom.

'Certainly!' said Pinkle politely. 'Please do! You won't find a single yellow trumpet here!'

And they didn't. Not one! But just as they were

going away again, feeling very puzzled, a pixie came running in.

'Come and see the lovely yellow flowers in the field!' he cried. 'They are wonderful! We've never seen anything like them before!'

Off went everyone to see them, and Pinkle and Flip were taken along too.

But when the fairies looked at them carefully, they saw what made the flowers look strange and beautiful – they each had a yellow trumpet in the middle of their petals!

'So *that's* where you hide them, you rascals!' cried the fairies, and caught hold of Pinkle and Flip angrily. 'Out of Fairyland you shall go!'

'No, no!' wept Pinkle and Flip miserably. 'Please let us stay. We'll never, never, NEVER make big yellow trumpets again!'

Suddenly a fairy had a great idea.

'I know!' he cried. 'Let's allow Pinkle and Flip to go on making their trumpets for these flowers! See how much more beautiful they are with the long trumpets in the middle!'

'Yes, yes!' cried all the fairies and pixies.

So it was settled. And from that day to this, Pinkle and Flip had to work hard to make the big yellow trumpets for the loveliest yellow flowers of the spring.

You have seen them often, for daffodils grow in everybody's garden – and if you look carefully at them next springtime, you will see how beautifully Pinkle and Flip have made their yellow trumpets.

Juggins the Giant

Juggins the Giant

ONCE UPON a time, a good many years ago now, there lived a giant called Juggins. He was rather stupid, but very strong and savage, and wherever he settled down to live the people became frightened and ran away.

Juggins was proud of his great strength. He boasted of it all day long, and dear me, he certainly was strong! He once leant against a house when he was tired, and down it went, clitter-clatter! Another time he stamped his foot in a rage and made a hole big enough to take a horse and cart! As for his voice, you could hear it a mile away, and people often thought a storm was coming when all the time it was simply Juggins shouting at his dog!

One day he came to live in the peaceful village of Hideaway. Juggins had heard that the finest, fattest pigs were grown there, and as he was very fond of bacon he thought it would be a splendid idea to go to Hideaway, settle down there and frighten the people into giving him bacon every day for breakfast.

Everyone was horrified when Juggins strode into their peaceful village, his hobnailed boots making a clatter like the noise of twelve wagons. They rushed to their doors and windows, and groaned when they saw Juggins.

'Now there will be no peace or happiness for anyone!' said High-Hat, the head of the village. 'This giant is a robber and a bully. We must put up with him as best we may.'

'Why should we put up with him?' cried Snippety, a small gnome in a red suit. 'Aren't you head of our village, High-Hat, and supposed to be clever enough to look after us and save us from people like this Giant Juggins?'

High-Hat frowned. Snippety was always saying things like that. High-Hat was lazy and didn't always do his duties well, and he was half afraid of the sharp little gnome Snippety.

'Hold your tongue,' said High-Hat to Snippety, frowning at him. 'I am about to call a meeting to decide what we shall do about Juggins.'

So the meeting was called – but nobody seemed to be able to think of anything that would send Juggins away. High-Hat rubbed his long nose and brought out his plan.

'Let us offer Juggins fifty pounds of our best bacon to go away,' he said. 'He is so fond of bacon that he will probably accept that and go. What do you think, friends?'

Everyone nodded his head and agreed mournfully – everyone, that is, except Snippety, who at once jumped to his feet and shouted, 'No! No!'

'And why do you say, "No! No!"?' asked High-Hat in a very cold voice.

'Because you are going to do the very thing that will make Juggins stay here longer than ever!' cried Snippety. 'As soon as he tastes fifty pounds of our best bacon, he will say to himself, "Ha! Delicious! Best bacon I've ever tasted in my life! I shall stay here for ever and make the people give me my breakfast every day of the year."'

All the little folk nodded their heads. 'Quite right, quite right!' they said more mournfully than ever.

'Well, since you are so clever, perhaps you will tell us how *you* would make the giant go?' said High-Hat in a very nasty sort of voice.

'Certainly, certainly!' said Snippety. 'Juggins is a strong and fierce giant, but he is very stupid. I think I could outwit him, if you will let me try!'

'Good for old Snippety!' cried everyone except High-Hat. 'Good old Snips! Always got an idea, haven't you, Snips?'

'Well, usually,' said Snippety, looking modest. 'It's better to wear a cap to keep your brains warm than to do what some people do – wear a high hat to hide an empty head!'

High-Hat nearly boiled over with rage, but everyone laughed so much that he couldn't make himself heard. He put on his high hat and stalked out of the room in disgust. Nobody minded him going at all. They all wanted to know what Snippety's plan was.

He told them. 'I shall challenge the giant to three feats of strength,' he said, 'and I shall beat him at every one of them! That will scare him so much that he will go and never come back again!'

'But, Snippety, the giant is *much* stronger than you!' cried the gnomes. 'He will beat you at everything and then he will probably eat you for your impudence.'

'Leave it to me, leave it to me,' said Snippety grandly. 'All *you've* got to do is to come and see the three tests of strength and cheer me for all you're worth when I win them.'

'Oh, we'll do that all right!' cried his friends, and after that the meeting broke up. Snippety went off to the hill where Juggins lived in a great cave, and called on him. The giant poked his head out of the cave, and even bold little Snippety felt a bit funny inside when he saw those great staring eyes and horrid big teeth.

'Good afternoon, Giant Juggins,' said Snippety, bowing politely. 'I am Snippety-Snappety-Snorum, the great and only strong man in the world. I may seem little to you, but my strength is marvellous. I can squeeze water from a stone and kick lightning from a rock!'

The giant blinked his big eyes in astonishment that such a little manikin could boast so loudly.

'Pooh!' he said. 'You do not know what you say! I am Juggins, the strongest giant in the world. I could break you in half just by curling my little finger round you.'

'I dare say you could!' said Snippety, taking a step

backwards, but not showing a bit of fear. 'Well, Juggins, what about seeing who is the stronger of us two, me or you?'

'What! Now, do you mean?' asked Juggins, preparing to crawl out of his cave.

'No, no,' said Snippety hastily. 'We must have people to judge between us and to say who wins. There must be a prize too. If you win, you shall have a hundred fat pigs – and if I win I can have the treasure you have hidden in that cave of yours!'

Juggins grinned. It sounded easy to him, and his mouth watered at the thought of a hundred pigs for his own.

'Very well,' he said. 'What shall the tests be?'

'Can you kick dust from a hard rock?' asked Snippety. 'I can!'

'So can I!' said the giant boastfully. 'I know I can kick more than you, so that shall be one test.'

'And can you squeeze water from cricket balls?' asked Snippety. 'I can!'

Juggins looked doubtful. 'Well,' he said, 'I've never had cricket balls big enough to try, but if *you* can, well *I* can, for certain sure!'

'Right,' said Snippety, 'that's test number two. Now for the last one. In our big pond there are two water turtles, great big chaps. I can pull one out on the end of a rope, even though he tries his best to pull against me. Could you pull the other out, do you think?'

'Of course!' said Juggins readily. 'You can go back and tell your friends that we will have these tests on Saturday, in the field near the pond. And, by the way, after I've beaten you I shall probably eat you. Have you thought of that?'

'Of course I haven't,' said Snippety, 'because, my dear fellow, you won't beat me! *Good* morning!'

The giant stared angrily after the cheeky gnome and made up his mind to punish him well when he got hold of him. But Snippety didn't seem to feel the giant's anger, and sauntered off gaily with his pointed cap well on one side.

He told his friends that Saturday was the day fixed for the three tests, and then he began to be very busy. He got out his tall boots and put them on the table in readiness. Then, curiously enough, he swept his chimney! He got a sack of soot from his chimney and looked pleased. Then he did a strange thing! He filled his boots almost up to the top with soot! He also took a pair of gloves and filled those with soot too. He grinned to himself as he did this, and chuckled loudly.

Next he went to order two large cricket balls to be made for the giant to squeeze – but he did not order any small ones for himself. No, he simply took two oranges and painted them very carefully with bright red paint and then put them on his windowsill to dry. They looked exactly like cricket balls when they were finished! Snippety was delighted.

The next thing he did was to buy two long pieces of stout rope, and when Saturday morning came he went down to the pond, very early, before anyone else was up. He whistled softly, and a large water turtle swam up to the surface.

'Hallo, Hardback!' said Snippety. 'Do me a favour, will you? Go and tie the end of this rope to that enormous old buried tree in the bottom of the pond – you know, the one that fell in twelve years ago when it was struck by lightning.'

The turtle took the rope and vanished. It came up again in two minutes and looked at Snippety with its small, bright eyes. It was fond of this cheeky gnome, who so often came to feed it.

'And now, Hardback,' said Snippety, 'just one more thing. You see this second rope, don't you? Well, tie it to the roots of a water plant, and listen hard for me to shout this morning. I shall pull this rope, and shout all the time. Don't take any notice of my shouting till you hear me say, "Now then, you miserable Hardback, come up with you!" Then you must make a great disturbance in the pond, untie the rope from the roots and hang on to it yourself. I shall then pull you out of the water. But don't untie the rope that is tied to the old tree, whatever you do!'

The turtle nodded its wrinkled head and took the second rope. It tied it carefully to the roots of a big water plant, and then popped its head out of the water to see what was going to happen.

At midday, when the sun was high, Giant Juggins came stalking down the hill. He looked very grand and very fierce, for he had on a feathered hat, a big cloak that flew out in the wind and a most enormous sword that glittered in the bright sunshine. Nobody felt brave when they saw him, not even Snippety – but he was plucky, and he went forward to greet the giant.

'Where are the hundred pigs?' asked Juggins, looking round. Now Snippety hadn't bothered about those, because he felt so certain of winning – but Juggins was angry to find that the prize was not there. So there was a great delay while a hundred fat pigs were rounded up and put into a ring of hurdles. They made a great squealing, and the giant looked at them with pleasure. What a lot of fat bacon!

'The first test is to see who can kick the most dust out of this big rock here,' said Snippety boldly. 'Have you brought your biggest boots, Giant Juggins?'

'Yes,' said the giant, and he took from his back a most enormous pair of high boots. He meant to do the thing well, and show everyone what a strong, fierce fellow he was. Ho, ho! How they would quail and shrink when they saw what he could do!

He put on his boots and went to stand on the great rock. Then he began to kick and stamp on it. My goodness me, what a noise, what a clatter, what a shower of rocky fragments and splinters!

But there was no dust at all. Sparks flew from beneath the giant's feet, and everyone fled out of reach of the bits of rock that flew up into the air. Smash, crash, clatter, smash, crash, clatter went the giant's feet. He was enjoying himself hugely.

'Well,' he said at last, quite out of breath. 'Is that

enough for you, good people? Have I shown you how to kick dust out of a rock?'

'That is hardly dust,' said Snippety, picking up a large piece of rock. 'Still, we will see if I can do any better. Yours was certainly a remarkable performance, Juggins!'

The small gnome slipped on his big, sooty boots, and put on his sooty gloves. Then he stepped on to the rock and began to kick and stamp. The soot flew up out of his boots and rose in a great black cloud!

'OooooooooOOOH!' cried everyone in the very greatest astonishment. Even Juggins was amazed, and opened his mouth wide in surprise. He got it full of soot and began to choke and cough.

'What a dust! What a dust!' cried all the watching folk. 'Ooh, Snippety, how marvellous you are! Look at all the dust you are kicking out of the rock!'

Snippety, quite hidden in a cloud of black soot, began to clap his gloved hands together. At once more soot flew out and the cloud round him was thicker and blacker than ever. He began to choke and cough too, but he wouldn't give up! No, he kicked and danced, stamped and shuffled on the rock till he hadn't an ounce of breath left. It was the others who stopped him.

'Stop, Snippety, stop!' they cried. 'You have won! Even Juggins says you have won! He did not kick dust as you do, he simply kicked the rock to pieces!'

So Snippety stopped and came down from the rock, smiling all over his very black and dirty face.

'I raised some dust, didn't I?' he said. 'I'll have to go and wash before we have the next test. I am really very dirty.'

Off he went and made himself clean. Then he picked up the two enormous cricket balls and the two small, painted oranges and set off to the field again, where the giant waited with everyone else.

'Test number two!' shouted Snippety grandly. 'Two cricket balls for you, Juggins, and two small ones for me, just the right size to fit our hands. Now then, stand over there opposite to me, and at the word "Go!" squeeze the balls as hard as you can!'

'One, two, three, *go*!' shouted High-Hat, when they were both ready. The giant squeezed his cricket balls and they became soft and flabby – but no water came from them. But to everyone's great amazement, juice came out of the two balls held by Snippety and dropped slowly to the ground!

'Look at Snippety!' cried the watching folk. 'See, he is squeezing yellow water out of the balls! Oh, how strong and clever he is! He has won the second test too!'

The giant squeezed his cricket balls harder than ever, but it was no use – not a drop came out of them, and no wonder either! In a temper he flung them into the air and they dropped into the pond with a splash! Snippety, half afraid that the giant might ask to see his balls, was only too glad to do the same – and splash they went into the pond, where they were eagerly gobbled up by the surprised water turtle!

'Now for the last test,' said Snippety, dancing up to the two ropes and giving the giant one of them. 'See who can pull his turtle out of the pond first!'

The giant took hold of his rope and strained hard at it, thinking to pull the water turtle out with a rush – but his rope was fastened to the long-sunk tree in the middle of the deep pond, and it barely stirred when he pulled. It was covered with mud, and had sunk deeply down.

Snippety pulled hard too, and danced about as he tugged, shouting, 'Come on, there! Hey, come on, there! Wait till I get you out of the water!'

But nothing came. The water turtle was listening for the right words, and all that happened was that Snippety's rope pulled hard at the roots of the water plant, but nothing else. Then the giant pulled his rope again. How he pulled! His face wrinkled up, his tongue stuck out, his forehead became wet – but no matter how he tried he could *not* pull a water turtle out of the water.

Snippety pulled on his rope again, and this time he shouted loudly, 'Now then, you miserable Hardback, come up with you!'

At once the listening turtle undid the rope from the plant's root and hung on to it himself. Snippety pulled hard and up came the water turtle out of the pond with the end of the rope in his mouth!

'Snippety's won, Snippety's won!' yelled everyone, dancing madly about in glee. 'He's stronger than Juggins the giant! He's a fine fellow is Snippety! He's better than a giant, so he is!'

Juggins stood listening to this, a great frown on his hot forehead. He was astonished when he saw the water turtle come up out of the pond. Why, it wasn't very big – and if that silly little Snippety could drag a little creature like that out of the pond, why, he could too!

He suddenly began to pull again. Snippety was alarmed, because he didn't want the giant to find out the trick he had played on him.

'You don't need to pull up your turtle,' he said at once. 'I've won, Juggins. Spare yourself.'

But the giant was furiously angry now, and he pulled like a hundred bulls. The buried tree in the pond shifted a little and gave way about two inches. The giant felt it giving and tugged again. The tree moved once more, and Snippety became very much alarmed.

'Stop, I tell you,' he cried to the giant. 'There is a fearful water creature in that pond, and perhaps it has got hold of your rope. If you pull it out, it will eat us all up, and you too.'

The giant stopped in fear – but soon his anger came upon him again and he tugged with all his strength. And then, with a fearful gurgling, sucking noise, that enormous old tree came up out of the pond! It had stiff, dripping branches that looked like hair, and the noise it made was most terrifying. Everyone shrieked in horror and tore off as fast as their legs would carry them.

'The water monster! The water monster! It will eat us all up! OoooooooooooOOOH!'

'Run! Run!' cried Snippety to the frightened giant, who really thought he had pulled up a great monster. 'It will eat you first. Run for your life!'

Juggins dropped the rope and tore off, taking a quarter of a mile in each stride. In no time at all he was a thousand miles away, vowing never, never, *never* to return to the village of Hideaway, with its awful Snippety and its terrible water monster!

As soon as he was gone, Snippety sat down and laughed till he cried. Then he called back the little folk and showed them that the monster was only the buried tree.

'We will dry it and cut it up for logs,' he said. 'Well, friends, am I not a smart gnome?'

'You are marvellous!' cried everyone, even High-Hat. 'You shall have all the giant's treasure from his cave and we will make you head of the village, Snippety. And now, do *do* tell us how you squeezed juice from the cricket balls and how you kicked such black dust from the rock.'

But Snippety looked very wise and shook his head. 'No,' he said. 'Those are my secrets. I shall never tell you.'

And he never did tell anyone but the old water turtle. The turtle told the frogs, and the frogs croaked the whole story out to one another in the springtime. So now everyone knows, even you!

Blue Shoes for the Party

Blue Shoes for the Party

'MUMMY!' CRIED Ann, dancing into the kitchen, where her mother was making cakes. 'I've got an invitation to Lucy's party. May I go?'

'If you're a good girl,' said her mother. 'You can wear your new blue dress.'

'But what about shoes?' asked Ann. 'I haven't any blue ones to match, Mummy. And my old party ones are no use now because they don't fit me.'

'Well, perhaps I'll buy you a new pair of blue ones,' said her mother. 'But you must just show me how good you can be, Ann, or I certainly shan't buy you any.'

Ann made up her mind to be as good as gold. But somehow or other things seemed to go wrong. Ann dropped one of her mother's very best cups and broke it. Then she dropped a bowl of flowers she was carrying, and that broke too, and all the water went on the carpet.

Ann's mother was cross.

'You're a careless little girl,' she said.

Ann said she was sorry. She did hope her mother wouldn't be cross enough not to buy her the blue shoes. She determined to be very careful indeed for the few days before the party.

Soon another unlucky thing happened. Ann lost her new socks! Then her mother was really cross!

'You'll have just one more chance!' she said to the little girl. 'If you do one more careless or naughty thing you shall not have your new shoes!'

Ann knew that her mother meant what she said, and she began to be really afraid she wouldn't be able to go to the party. So for the next two days she was a very good little girl indeed.

Then came the day before the party.

'Mummy, may I go and buy those new blue shoes with you?' asked Ann.

'Yes,' said her mother. 'I'll take you this afternoon. But this morning I want you to take a message for me to Mrs Robinson. Here is the note. Now go straight there and back. You just have got time before lunch, so don't dawdle as you did last time. If you do, lunch will be cold, and we shall probably miss the only bus into the town to get your shoes.'

'All right, Mummy!' said Ann happily. 'I'll be sure to be back in time!'

Off she ran with the note. She went down the lane, and over the stile into the fields. Soon she came to the wood, and took the path that ran through it. She didn't stop for anything, not even when she saw some lovely foxgloves blooming all together.

When she arrived at Mrs Robinson's Ann gave her the note, took the answer and turned to go home again.

I shall be home before Mummy expects me! she thought.

Now, as she went back through the wood she chanced to hear a cry. It was a funny sort of sound, not like a bird or animal. Ann wondered what it could be. She stopped a moment, and looked through the trees where she thought the cry had come from. And as she stopped someone came running out from the trees towards her.

Ann stared in surprise – for it was an elf! He was very small, tinier than Ann, and he was crying.

'Little girl, little girl,' he cried, 'come and help me! My butterflies are all entangled in the thorns!'

Ann ran through the trees to where he pointed. There she saw an astonishing sight. There was a beautiful little carriage, drawn by five blue butterflies, but somehow or other they had got themselves caught in a bramble bush, and their pretty wings were being torn as they struggled to free themselves.

'Could you help me?' asked the elf, drying his eyes. 'If you could hold the reins tightly I think I could get their wings free. But it will take rather a long time.'

'Oh, dear!' said Ann in dismay. 'I'd love to help you, little elf, but my mother says I must get home quickly. You see, she's going to take me into town to buy me a pair of blue shoes for tomorrow's party, and if I'm late she won't take me, and anyhow we should miss the bus. I'm afraid I can't stop to help you.'

'All right,' said the elf, tears streaming down his face again. 'I quite understand. But, oh, my poor butterflies! They'll be torn to bits. If you meet another little girl who hasn't got to buy shoes for the party, will you tell her to come and help me?'

Ann looked at him, and then looked at the butterflies. She knew quite well that she wouldn't meet anyone else going through the woods. She didn't know what to do.

Then she suddenly made up her mind.

'Don't cry,' she said. 'I'll stay and help. Perhaps I'll be in time for lunch after all.'

'Oh, thank you a thousand times!' cried the elf,

wiping his eyes. 'Come on then. Hold the reins, and I'll go and calm the butterflies.'

Ann climbed into the little carriage, and held the reins firmly. The elf ran to his butterflies and began to disentangle their wings from the cruel thorns. One by one he freed them. It took a long time, for he was so afraid of tearing their beautiful wings. But at last it was done.

'There!' he said joyfully. 'They're all free now. Thank you so much, little girl. I do hope you'll be in time.'

'I hope so too,' said Ann. 'Well, goodbye and I hope you get home safely.'

She ran off. She knew it must be very late. She ran faster than she had ever run before. She panted and puffed, and didn't stop once till she reached home and ran up the garden path.

'Well!' said her mother. 'What in the world have you been doing to be so late? Lunch is over long ago and the bus is just starting.'

'Oh, Mummy!' said Ann, nearly crying. 'I really couldn't help it. You see, I met an elf and–'

'Nonsense!' said her mother crossly. 'You've been dawdling again. Well, you can't have your blue shoes, that's all.'

'But, Mummy, I can't go to the party unless I have them!' said Ann. 'I haven't any others I can wear.'

'Well, it's your own fault!' said her mother. 'You're a silly little girl. Now go and eat your lunch, and don't let me hear a word more.'

Poor Ann! She went and sat down at the table, but she couldn't eat anything. She was so dreadfully disappointed. She saw the bus go off, and a big lump came into her throat. No shoes and no party! She was very sad.

She had to look after the baby all the afternoon, and after tea she had some schoolwork to do. She went early to bed, for she wanted to go to sleep and forget her disappointment.

Early the next morning she got up to get her mother

a cup of tea. She opened the front door of the cottage to bring in the milk – and then she stopped and stared in surprise.

On the doorstep was a box. It was bright yellow, and tied with blue ribbon. A small label hung from it that said: FOR THE LITTLE GIRL WHO HELPED MY BUTTERFLIES.

Ann picked up the box. She quickly took off the ribbon and opened the lid. And, oh my! What do you think was inside? Why, the prettiest, daintiest pair of blue satin shoes you could possibly imagine, and instead of buckles they had two tiny blue butterflies, just like the big ones she had helped the day before.

Ann cried out with joy. She sat down on the doorstep and tried the shoes on. They fitted her exactly – and didn't they look lovely! They were the prettiest pair she had ever seen in her life, far, far nicer than any she could have bought in a shop.

She ran upstairs to her mother.

'Mummy, Mummy!' she cried. 'Look, the elf has

brought me some shoes for the party! I expect he knew that I couldn't go and buy any because he made me late!'

Then, of course, her mother had to hear all the story, and she was very glad when she knew what had happened.

'Well, you deserve them,' she said to Ann. 'I really didn't believe you had met an elf, but I do now, for these shoes are fairy ones, if ever shoes were! You will look lovely in them!'

'Hurrah!' said Ann. 'Everything has come right now! I shall enjoy the party!' And she did!

The Boy With a Thousand Wishes

The Boy With a Thousand Wishes

THERE WAS once a sharp boy called Gordon. He longed and longed to meet a brownie or a pixie, or someone belonging to the little folk, because he wanted to ask for a wish.

'Just one wish,' said Gordon to himself. 'Only just one! Surely they wouldn't mind me having just one.'

Well, his chance came one morning when he was walking so quietly that a brownie who was sitting under a bush, half asleep, didn't see him until Gordon was right on top of him. The brownie tried to scramble away into the bush – but Gordon put out a long arm and caught him.

'A brownie at last!' said Gordon, pleased. 'Good! No, it's no use struggling – you can't get away!'

The brownie stopped struggling at once. He was a tiny fellow, only just as high as Gordon's knee, and his eyes were as green as moss in the sunlight. His beard almost reached the ground.

'Let me go,' begged the brownie.

'What will you give me if I do?' asked Gordon, keeping a tight hold of the little fellow.

'What do you want?' asked the green-eyed brownie sulkily.

'I want a wish,' said Gordon firmly.

'A wish! Just one wish?' said the brownie in surprise. 'Most people ask for three.'

'One wish will do very well for me,' said Gordon. The brownie stood straight up and looked closely into Gordon's eyes.

'Take my advice and do not ask for a wish,' he said. 'You'll be sorry!'

'I want a wish,' said Gordon. He shook the little

fellow hard. 'Now, hurry up, or I'll take you home with me.'

'You can have your wish,' said the brownie, and his eyes gleamed like green stones. 'Let me go!'

'Not till I've wished my wish!' said Gordon. 'And this is what I wish – that I may have a wish granted every hour of the day and night!'

The brownie pulled himself free and began to laugh. 'You think you're clever, but you're not!' he called in his high little voice. 'Have all your wishes – but you'll be sorry!'

He disappeared behind a tree. Gordon rubbed his hands in glee. He felt quite sure that he would never be sorry.

'I wonder nobody has ever thought of this before!' he said to himself as he went home. 'One magic wish can bring as many other wishes as I like! Why people ask for three and then just use them for three silly things and no more puzzles me! Now I can have a wish granted every single hour!'

It was a long way home, and Gordon felt tired. He stood still and thought. 'I don't see why I shouldn't have my first wish now!' he said. 'Well, I wish for a fine motorcar to take me home!'

There was a bang – and out of the air appeared a red motorcar! At the wheel sat a fat gnome with a most unpleasant face. He grinned at Gordon.

'Good morning!' he said. 'I'm your wish gnome. I have to grant you a wish every single hour. The very first time you forget I'll take you off with me, and you shall be my slave! Then you will have to do my wishes!'

'You be careful, or I'll wish you away!' said Gordon sharply.

'Well, if you do that, your wishes won't come true any more, because I'm the fellow that grants them!' said the gnome. 'Now hop in and I'll take you home!'

Gordon hopped in. He thought it was a pity that he had to have a wish gnome to grant his wishes. When he got home his mother and father, brothers and sisters were most astonished to hear his story and see his fine new car.

'Wish me a silk frock!' cried Elaine.

'Wish me a car like yours!' cried John.

'Wish me, wish me, wish me . . .' shouted everyone.

'I'll wish what I like,' said Gordon. 'Be quiet, everyone! I shall have twenty-four wishes each day and night, and I will wish us riches, a castle, servants and anything else we want. This gnome is my wish gnome and he has to grant all my wishes!'

Well, all that day, each hour that came, Gordon wished. He wished for a castle. Bang! It appeared on the hill nearby! The whole family went to see it and chose their own rooms.

He wished for servants. Bang! They all appeared, one after the other, bowing low. He wished for money to buy fine food. Bang! A great purse of gold appeared in his hand, and Gordon sent the servants out to buy meat, fish, eggs, cakes, biscuits – everything he could think of! What a feast they all had!

By the time it was eight o'clock, Gordon had the castle, servants, gold, fine suits and dresses for everyone, a car for each of them, a throne of gold and a bed of silver. He had never felt so grand in all his life.

He was very tired with all the excitement. 'I'm going to bed,' he said to the wish gnome. 'Wake me at eight o'clock tomorrow.'

'But you have to wish a wish each hour of the night!' said the gnome. 'Don't you remember that you wished for a wish to be granted every single hour of the day and night?'

'Good gracious! Surely you don't mean I've got to wake up every hour and wish!' cried Gordon. 'I'll save them all up and wish twelve wishes tomorrow morning.'

'Oh, no, you won't,' said the gnome with a grin. 'You'll just keep to what you said. I'll wake you up each hour to wish.'

So poor Gordon had to wake up each hour and wish

something. He was so sleepy that it was difficult to think of things. He wished for a golden bicycle, a cat with blue eyes, a goldfish in a big bowl, three singing birds and many other things.

The next day he went on wishing. He wished himself a crown. He wished himself a kingdom. He wished his mother a golden ring with big diamonds in it. He wished his father a pipe rimmed with precious stones.

His brothers and sisters quarrelled about his wishes. They were always wanting him to wish something for them, and they could never wait their turn.

'Oh, do stop quarrelling!' begged Gordon. 'I should have thought that being so rich, and having such wonderful things to wear and to eat, you would have been very happy. Instead, you quarrel and fight, and disturb me all the time.'

It was such a nuisance having to wake up each night and wish every hour. 'I really can't be bothered to wake up tonight,' said Gordon to the wish gnome one night. 'I'll go without my wishes.'

'Gordon, if you do that, you'll be in my power and I'll whisk you away!' cried the gnome in delight.

Gordon looked at the gnome. He couldn't bear him. 'How can I get rid of you?' he asked. 'I really don't feel as if I want anything else now, and it's a great nuisance to have to think of a wish every hour!'

'You can only get rid of me if you ask me to do something I can't do!' said the wish gnome, grinning. 'But as I can grant every wish, it's not likely you'll be able to do that. I shall just stay with you till you get so tired of wishing that you'll stop – and then I shall whisk you away and make you do my wishes.'

So poor Gordon went on and on wishing each day and night. He longed to get rid of the gnome. He set him all kinds of impossible things to do – but the gnome did them all!

Gordon wished for seven blue elephants with yellow ears. He was sure there were none in the world! But the gnome brought them all right, and very peculiar they looked, standing in the courtyard, waving their blue trunks about!

It didn't matter what the boy wished, his wishes came true. And all the time his family squabbled and fought, each trying to get Gordon's wishes for themselves.

'Wish me a new white horse!' screamed Fanny.

'Wish me three black dogs!' shouted Ken.

'Wish me a more comfortable bed!' cried Elaine.

'You be quiet, Elaine! It's my turn to have a wish!' said John fiercely, and he pulled Elaine's hair. She slapped his face. He ran after her, and she bumped into Gordon, knocking him down. John trod on him.

Gordon leapt to his feet in a rage. 'How dare you! How dare you!' he yelled. 'I'm a king! I won't have you treating me like this!'

'Pooh! You're only Gordon really!' said Elaine rudely.

'Oh, I am, am I?' said Gordon fiercely. 'Well, you're only Elaine. I wish all my wishes undone! May everything be as it was before! I'm tired of all this!'

Bang! The castle vanished. The servants disappeared. Their rich clothes became the poor ones of before. The whole family found themselves in their cottage, staring in fear and surprise at one another.

'Serves you right!' said Gordon. 'You don't deserve good fortune. You were much nicer when you were poor and hard-working. And so was I!'

He sat with his head in his hand, unhappy and puzzled. To think that he had all the wishes in the world and yet was not so happy as when he had none! It was too bad.

In an hour's time the wish gnome appeared, grinning. 'Well!' he said. 'Do you want to wish your castle back?'

'No, I don't,' said Gordon. He snatched a boiling kettle off the stove. 'Freeze this boiling water!' he said. 'Go on! I'm hot and I want ice to suck. Freeze this hot water.'

Well, the gnome did everything he could to make

that water freeze, but of course he couldn't. No one can make hot water into ice – it just won't happen!

The gnome threw down the kettle, looking angry. 'It can't be done!' he said. 'It's impossible. Wish something else that I can do, or I shall disappear for ever and you won't be able to have another wish come true all your life long.'

'Then disappear!' cried Gordon. 'Go! I don't want any more wishes!'

Bang! The gnome went – and that was the last time Gordon ever saw him. No more of his wishes came true – but he didn't care! It was a better thing to live happily in a cottage with his family, and to work hard, and laugh, than to live in a huge castle with nothing to do but quarrel and fight.

'I thought I was so sharp, only asking for one wish in order to have thousands,' said Gordon to himself. 'But I was stupid! I'll never do it again.'

He needn't worry. He won't get the chance!

The Crown of Gold

The Crown of Gold

ONCE UPON a time there was a fairy who was very sad. He sat in a yellow celandine, and swayed to and fro, thinking about everything. Two big tears rolled down his cheeks and trickled down the stalk of the celandine.

'Oh, dear, oh, dear!' he sighed.

'Whatever is the matter?' said a brimstone butterfly, out for the first time that spring.

'Oh,' answered Casilda, the little fairy, 'I'm sad because I don't do anything so well as the other fairies can. I can't make beautiful dresses from morning mist like Sylfai, I can't paint the sunset pink, and I can't even hang the dewdrops on the grasses without spilling them.'

'That is very sad,' said the butterfly. 'But what does it matter?'

'Well, you see,' explained Casilda, 'every summer our king holds his court, and give little silver crowns set with pearls to all those fairies who do beautiful work. *All* my friends have got crowns, but I never win one, however hard I try.'

'Cheer up,' said the butterfly, 'there are other things worthwhile doing, even if you don't win a crown for them!'

'Oh, *what*?' exclaimed Casilda.

'Why, go into the world of boys and girls and see if you can't help the people there a bit,' said the butterfly. 'There are always lots of things to be done, even if you can't do them really well.'

'I'll go at once!' cried Casilda, standing up in the swaying celandine. 'Goodbye, yellow butterfly, and thank you!' Off he flew, out of Fairyland and into our world.

The first thing he came to there was a clothesline pegged with clothes. Mr Wind was tugging at one beautiful frock, and trying his hardest to pull it down into the mud.

'You *are* in a bad mood today, Mr Wind!' cried Casilda. He flew on to the clothesline, and sat down by the frock, holding it tight. Mr Wind tugged and tugged, and very nearly made the little fairy tumble off. Then out of the house hobbled an old woman.

When she saw Casilda she cried out with pleasure. 'Oh, thank you,' she said, 'if you hadn't held the frock on the line for me, little fairy, the wind would have whisked it away, and I should have had to wash it clean again. My poor old back is tired of stooping to wash, so thank you very much.'

'Don't mention it,' called Casilda, flying off again.

The next day Casilda heard a tiny child crying bitterly because his balloon had blown away, and he could not reach it.

'Never mind,' said Casilda. 'Watch me get it!' And off he flew up into the air, caught the string and flew down again. The balloon came down with the string, and the child was delighted.

'Oh, thank you, dear little fairy,' he said gratefully.

'Don't mention it,' said Casilda, flying away.

Another time Casilda, peeping in at a window of a little house, saw a woman crying. She was holding her head, and saying, 'Oh, my head *does* hurt so.'

Whatever can I do for her? thought Casilda. *I can't think of anything*. He looked round the room and noticed how dirty and dark it was.

I know, he thought, *the room wants brightening up. I'll get some flowers.*

Off he flew to the meadows, and brought back a lovely bunch of golden buttercups and white daisies. He dropped them into the woman's lap. She was so astonished that she stopped crying, and forgot all about her bad headache.

'How lovely!' she cried. 'And how dark and dirty

the room looks now with these bright flowers in it. I must hurry up and clean it.'

So she put the flowers in water, and started cleaning the room, singing cheerfully.

Casilda flew away feeling very pleased with himself. 'Tomorrow is the day our king holds his court and gives those lovely crowns,' he said to himself. 'I shall have to go, but I shan't mind a bit not winning a crown, because I've found something else I can do to make myself happy.'

Every fairy came to the king's palace the next day. The king was on his throne, and by him were many little silver crowns set with pearls. There was also one little golden crown set with diamonds, and Casilda wondered whether any of his friends had won it.

'Do you think you've won a crown this year?' asked Sylfai, the fairy dressmaker.

'Oh, no,' answered Casilda, 'I know I haven't, because I've stopped doing beautiful things, and I live in the world of boys and girls now.'

Then the king made a speech, and said how glad he was to have the crowns to give to fairies who had done beautiful things that year.

'Peronel,' he called. 'Here is a crown for you. You did a most beautiful thing when you painted the almond blossom such a lovely pink this spring.'

Peronel proudly received the crown.

'Morfael,' said the king. 'This crown is given to you for ringing the bluebells so sweetly at our last dance.'

Morfael went up for his crown most delighted. Then one by one the king gave out all his crowns except the gold one.

'This crown,' he said, 'is for a little fairy who gave up doing beautiful things in Fairyland, but went all by himself into the world of boys and girls and did beautiful things there. He didn't think they were beautiful, but they were, and we are very proud of him. Casilda, here is your crown.'

You can just imagine how pleased Casilda was,

and what a lovely surprise he had. He is the only fairy in Fairyland who wears a golden crown, so if you meet a fairy wearing one, you will know at once that it is Casilda.

The Green Goblin

The Green Goblin

THERE WAS once a green goblin who thought himself very clever indeed. He thought he ought to be king of all the goblins, but nobody liked him enough to crown him.

One day the green goblin found a curious old book and in it were the directions for a very powerful spell. This is what the goblin read in the book: 'Take as many peas as four times seven, as many green feathers as six times six, and a half-score of little blue worms; say the magic word which the witches use each Saturday night to make their broomsticks fly; you will find it if you take the fourth of February, the first of October, the middle of Christmas, the second of January, the third of November and the beginning of the year; stir the peas and the blue worms with the feathers as many times as there are days in June. Then will appear a little yellow spell, which, when looked at carefully for two minutes by a green goblin, will make him king of all the rest.'

Now when the green goblin read this he was most excited. Just the spell he wanted! He felt sure he could easily do it. So, my dears, he took out his notebook and began to work out the spell. This is what he put:

Take four times seven peas which is twenty-eight.
Take six times six green feathers, which is thirty.
Take a half-score of blue worms, which is ten.
Say the witch word, which is Uotavy.
Stir thirty-one times.

The goblin rubbed his hands in glee. He was pleased to have worked out the spell so quickly.

'I am clever, clever, clever!' he sang. 'I shall soon

be king of all the goblins. I deserve it! I shall wear a green crown and a black cloak and I shall command this and that! I shall say, "Off with their heads!" if I am not obeyed! Oh, I will have a wonderful time!'

Well, you can see he wasn't a very nice goblin, really, although he thought himself clever. He set to work to make the spell. He shelled twenty-eight peas from their pods. He bought thirty green feathers from a parrot. He dug up ten blue worms from the garden. Then he said, 'Uotavy' very solemnly and stirred the peas and the worms with the green feathers thirty-one times.

He waited for the spell to appear. It came at last – but instead of being yellow it was purple, and had two pink spots, one at each end. The goblin was puzzled at first, but thought it wouldn't really matter.

'Now I'll take it to the other goblins,' he said to himself, 'and look at it carefully for two minutes. Ho ho! At the end of that time I'll be their king and wear a crown and a royal cloak! I'll make them all bow and scrape to me, yes I will!'

Off he went, carrying the spell. The other goblins were at work in their cave and were most astonished to see the green goblin appear with something in his hand, at which he stared very solemnly for two whole minutes.

Well, do you know, a very queer thing happened at the end of that time – the goblin grew two long ears, and grey fur all over his body! The others stared in surprise and then they began to laugh. 'He's turned himself into a little grey donkey!' they cried. 'Oh, how suitable! He always *was* a silly little donkey, although he thought himself so clever. He's made a spell and done it wrong! Ho, ho, ho!'

And so he had! He had made mistakes in that very simple spell, and the magic he had made was for a donkey and not for a king! Can *you* find his mistakes? See if you can do the spell right – but remember, it won't turn *you* into a king, because you don't happen to be a green goblin!

Acknowledgements

All efforts have been made to seek necessary permissions. The stories in this publication first appeared in the following publications:

'The Magic Rubber' first appeared in *Enid Blyton's Sunny Stories*, No. 55, 1938.

'Dame Roundy's Stockings' first appeared in *Enid Blyton's Sunny Stories*, No. 313, 1943.

'A Spell for a Puppy' first appeared in *Sunny Stories for Little Folks*, No. 245, 1936.

'Briony and the Naughty Fairies' first appeared in *Teachers World*, No. 916, 1922.

'The Fairy Kitten' first appeared in *The Teacher's Treasury*, Vol. 1, 1926.

'The Talking Teapot' first appeared in *Sunny Stories for Little Folks*, No. 95, 1930.

'The Brownies' Party' first appeared in *Enid Blyton's Sunny Stories*, No. 10, 1937.

'Fee-Fi-Fo the Goblin' first appeared in *Sunny Stories for Little Folks*, No. 212, 1935.

'Dan's Magic Gold' first appeared in *Teachers World*, No. 890, 1922.

'The Fool and the Magician' first appeared in *Teachers World*, Nos. 20 and 27 in 1933.

'The Midnight Elves' first appeared in *Sunny Stories for Little Folks*, No. 87, 1930.

'One Bonfire Night' first appeared in *Enid Blyton's Magazine*, No. 23, 1957.

'The Wind's Party' first appeared in *Sunday Mail* (Glasgow), No. 1,881, 1944.

'The Brownie Who Thought He Was Clever' first appeared in *The Teacher's Treasury*, Vol. 1, 1926.

'Peronel and His Pot of Glue' first appeared in *Teachers World*, No. 885, 1922.

'The Magic Knitting Needles' first appeared in *Enid Blyton's Sunny Stories*, No. 83, 1938.

'The Wicked Witch' first appeared in *Teachers World*, No. 986, 1923.

'Games in Goblin Land' first appeared in *Sunny Stories for Little Folks*, No. 246, 1936.

'Sneezing Powder' first appeared in *Enid Blyton's Sunny Stories*, No. 132, 1939.

'Billy's Little Boats' first appeared in *Enid Blyton's Sunny Stories*, No. 132, 1938.

'The Little Green Imp' first appeared in *Enid Blyton's Sunny Stories*, No. 62, 1938.

'The Wishing Hat' first appeared as 'The Wizard's Hat' in *Sunny Stories for Little Folks*, No. 160, 1933.

'The Kickaway Shoes' first appeared in *Sunny Stories for Little Folks*, No. 166, 1933.

'The Witch's Cat' first appeared in *Enid Blyton's Sunny Stories*, No. 356, 1945.

'The Yellow Trumpets' first appeared in *The Teacher's Treasury*, Vol. 1, 1926.

'Juggins the Giant' first appeared in *Sunny Stories for Little Folks*, No. 213, 1935.

'Blue Shoes for the Party' first appeared in *Sunny Stories for Little Folks*, No. 93, 1930.

'The Boy With a Thousand Wishes' first appeared in *Enid Blyton's Sunny Stories*, No. 181, 1940.

'The Crown of Gold' first appeared as 'The Fairy's Crown' in *Merry Moments*, Vol. 4, 1922.

'The Green Goblin' first appeared in *Teachers World*, No. 1,702, 1936.

Also available:

A spellbinding selection of magical and mischievous tales by the world's best-loved storyteller!

THE SECRET SEVEN

READ ALL 15 CLASSIC STORIES!

Enid Blyton®

THE

SECRET SEVEN

SOLVE THE MYSTERY!

Don't miss…

Two action-packed Secret Seven stories from prizewinning author **PAMELA BUTCHART**!

Enid Blyton®

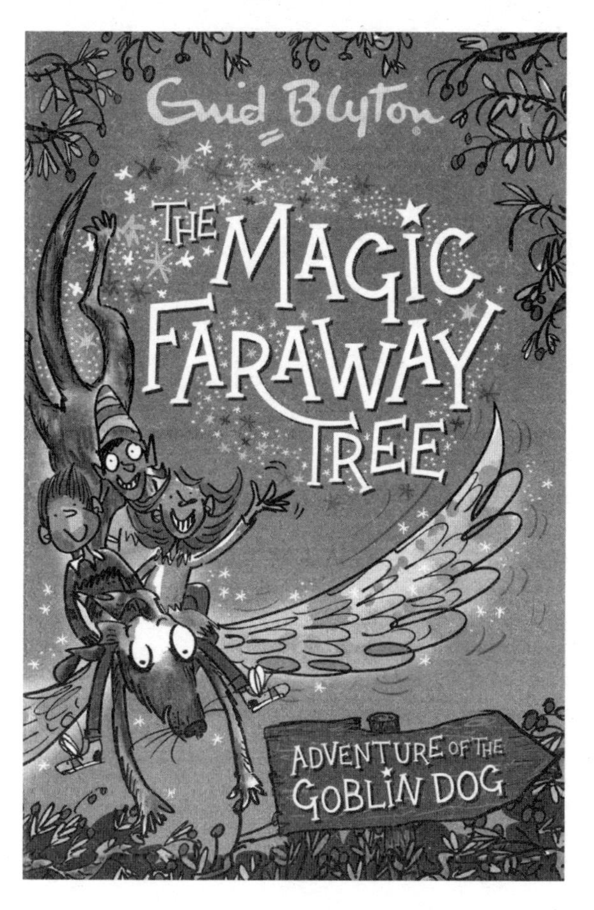

Discover the magic in this original
Magic Faraway Tree story by the world's best-loved
storyteller Enid Blyton!

Enid Blyton®

is one of the most popular children's authors of all time. Her books have sold over 500 million copies and have been translated into other languages more often than any other children's author.

Enid Blyton adored writing for children. She wrote over 700 books and about 2,000 short stories. *The Famous Five* books, now 75 years old, are her most popular. She is also the author of other favourites including *The Secret Seven*, *The Magic Faraway Tree*, *Malory Towers* and *Noddy*.

Born in London in 1897, Enid lived much of her life in Buckinghamshire and loved dogs, gardening and the countryside. She was very knowledgeable about trees, flowers, birds and animals. Dorset – where some of the Famous Five's adventures are set – was a favourite place of hers too.

Enid Blyton's stories are read and loved by millions of children (and grown-ups) all over the world. Visit enidblyton.co.uk to discover more.